LADY SCANDAL

A STEAMY REGENCY ROMANTIC COMEDY

LARISSA LYONS

Literary Madness!

The revised edition of Lady Scandal is dedicated to Martinique and Christina, two friends whose enthusiasm for joy-filled living enhances my own. Thank you both! Larissa

Published by Literary Madness
First Paperback Edition: June 2020
First Large Print Edition: July 2021
Second E-book Edition: June 2020

ISBN 978-0-9834711-6-5 Paperback
ISBN 978-1-949426-25-0 Large Print - July 2021
ISBN 978-1-949426-14-4 E-book (Rev. May 2021)

Proofread by Judy Zweifel at Judy's Proofreading; Edited by Elizabeth St. John; Copy edits by ELF at elewkf1@yahoo.com; Cover by Literary Madness

At Literary Madness, we strive to create a book free of typos. If you notice anything amiss, we're happy to fix it. litmadness@yahoo.com

CONTENTS

LADY SCANDAL

LADY SCANDAL

That's honest, by heavens! I am glad you are no enemy to matrimony.

— JANE AUSTEN, *NORTHANGER ABBEY*

PROLOGUE ~ THE MARRIAGE SCHEME

Though Lord Letheridge applied himself with undue diligence, groping and grabbing, fumbling for a feel of his young bride every chance he could, it was all for naught. By the time he'd wed his sixth and final wife, his body refused to cooperate. So, when Lord Letheridge died without legal issue, many of his sizable properties, the unentailed ones won gambling during his mis-begotten life, went to his dear wife. As did their debts.

Once funds and options were exhausted, the ever-practical Juliet, the heretofore perfectly proper and dutiful daughter (not to mention reluctantly willing wife, for all the good it never did), decided to take her future, and that of those dependent upon her, into her own creative hands.

For after seeing the hash her husband had made of things, Juliet was convinced a mere female could do no worse.

WANTED: A man for matrimony. One with well-equipt pockets.

Ideal candidates must possess blunt and plenty of it; not be overly fond of gaming nor drink. Fair of form and fine of face not essential (but certainly appreciated).

Comprehensive knowledge of estate management a boon.

In return, the chosen applicant will receive a genteel, amiable wife ready to bear his children. Female in question is of sound intellect and generally appealing countenance, is accomplished in many feminine arts, and not at all adverse to quiet evenings at home (once the roof leaks are repaired).

To be placed into your safekeeping and control upon formal marriage: rippling good lands covering parts of four distinct shires, three amazingly rundown properties, near-starving tenants, and sizable taxes due (currently in arrears).

Apply in person with all due haste to Mr. Bamber Hastings, Solicitor, village of Duffield, Derbyshire.

Applicants must supply verification of their financial worth, a vicar's declaration of their moral caliber, a physician's assertion of their state of health and vigor and lack of disease. Also have obtained three personal characters, including one from an inamorata stating, with no amount of equivocation, prowess pertaining to performing duties of an intimate nature.

THE NOTICE SCANDALIZED THE TON. *The Times* refused to run it, only taking up the story after the advertisement appeared in several lesser papers and—appropriately named—scandal sheets.

This is the tale of applicant twenty-four...

1

APPLICANT TWENTY-FOUR

UNTIL RECENT MONTHS, Zeus J. Tanner counted of value four things: money, time, his mother, and regaining his stolen birthright.

When his mum passed away after a brief illness and unexpectedly pleasant marriage, Zeus' list dwindled to three. Time, which gained the top rank when he realized how very much he wished they'd had more together. Money. Birthright.

The first he'd been forced to squander when his initial, hard-earned interview with "Lady

Scandal", as she'd been dubbed in London, was inexplicably postponed.

The second provided him comfortable lodgings at the Crown & Cup, the nearest inn to the Duffield solicitor who refused to divulge the location of today's interview until "absolutely necessary", just as he'd refused to justify the delay.

Ah, the pernickety solicitor. Mr. Bamber Hastings was not unknown to Zeus. In fact, it was his name in particular that had drawn Zeus to read the entire advertisement. The *contents* of the appallingly intriguing notice itself earned his presence here in Derbyshire.

Duffield, Derbyshire. He'd sworn never to return after his last inquiry—some years prior and conducted *through* Hastings—was met with substantial disdain.

But though they had a past history, albeit a brief one, Zeus didn't think Hastings had shown him any favor, scrutinizing his letters of validation with his quizzing glass amid indecipherable *harrumphs* and *tut-tuts*, until, finally, granting Zeus a line on Lady Scandal's appointment card.

One he'd had to cool his heels a good week before fulfilling, thanks to that yet-to-be-accounted-for delay.

Though the serving wenches at the Crown & Cup were willing to serve up themselves—and made that excessively clear to Zeus time and again—he'd not sampled their charms.

Nor been overly tempted to.

While a frolicking frisk with a fulsome wench might prove desirous for some, Zeus prided himself on mastering his baser urges. Stifling the compulsion to dip his wick in just any old—or young—wench with a willing wax pot, no matter how eminently swive-worthy their exterior might appear.

And that was because of Things He Valued #3—his stolen birthright. Or as he preferred to think of it...Amherst.

For if Lady Scandal proved to be who Zeus suspected, given her list of what she provided in exchange for money and loads of it, the unwilling prodigal would at last have a home. His own.

And the thought of finally realizing *that* particular satisfaction could warm a man on any number of cold nights, in any manner of cold, empty beds.

For Zeus was determined to regain what he considered his, and if he had to forsake flipping coins to beddable, buxom dells and palm his staff night after night, he'd do it and gladly. And he'd tell his randy prick to quit offering up complaints each time a serving wench brushed against his arm, or parts decidedly lower.

Juliet had been married, under protest, to an old goat who spent more time grazing beneath her skirts than he did tending his tenants. More time prodding between her thighs than he did taking his place in Parliament.

More time barking orders at everyone in his household—including her—than following his doctor's dictates.

So, when the esteemed—at least in everyone else's eyes—Lord Letheridge collapsed in a heap after devouring his third helping of glazed duck, Juliet did nothing more than nod, finish her *first* serving, and ring for dessert.

Oh, who was she hoaxing with that version?

Though Juliet might like to wish she possessed such strength of character, in truth, upon seeing her soused spouse slouch face-first into his ravaged duck bones, Juliet had shrieked, rushed to his side, and screamed for the butler.

But all of Leth's vices had stolen the vitality from his viscerals, rendering him nothing but a dustman. Rendering Juliet, she'd dimly realized, free of his fumbling. But not of his responsibilities.

Now, some fourteen months and as many assorted disasters later, Juliet remained determined not to let Fate or fatalistic happenings cast her down. And she'd certainly had a lot of practice, given how a carelessly placed candle caused her very home to go up in flames, and how her father recently attempted to wed her to yet another titled old codger with no advance warning (only this one had the good grace to expire on the journey up from Weymouth, thank the saints). And again when a series of tremors caused the well to cave in at another estate, a shockingly sudden occurrence, and her with no funds to hire someone willing to "dig" her out of the resulting predicament.

After the well ran figuratively and literally dry, she'd retreated to her last remaining option and current abode. As had happened with a number of the applicants, she'd learned what often presented itself well on paper didn't always convey in person.

Set amidst a respectable copse of trees and a good distance from any neighbors, the century-old home she now inhabited might be greeting her with falling plaster and broken hinges each time she entered a room, but just as they'd learned to tack the roof tiles back in place (the ones they could locate, that was) and prop the working windows open on boards, Juliet took it upon herself to shore up the spirits of everyone around her. As "lady" of the manor, she was determined to right the wrongs Leth's spendthrift ways had saddled her with.

To that end, once her viable options ran as dry as the well, Juliet turned to the unviable ones, consulting with Leth's rather haughty but surprisingly helpful solicitor and ultimately placing her advertisement. Only to have the disasters continue, with her lady's maid running off with the head groom (and taking the few remaining horses with them), the butler fleeing for greener (and irrigated) pastures, and herself, hosting the most recent adversity directly upon her person in the form of a broken bone in one of her lower limbs, thanks in no small part to an unintentional altercation with several uninvited barking barkers.

Dogs. She might have liked them once upon a dog day, but after hobbling around on one foot because of the four-legged fiends, her opinion of canines had taken a decisively downward turn. She now prayed Providence would do the opposite, take an upward turn and smile—instead of smirk—on her today by sending the right man into the sanctum of her sitting room.

Not a single applicant thus far had come close to reaching the vision she'd created of a respectable and worthy man intent on delivering them from penury. And her from another marriage not of her choosing.

But that's what came with having the misfortune of being sired by a man still mired in medieval times, one who thought he had the right to command her obedience in all things, regardless of her age. She'd witnessed that enough times with how he treated her mother. Despite no longer residing under her father's roof, Juliet had no doubt if she were unlucky enough to ever land there again, he would assume absolute power over everything she did, and that was not to be borne.

She might not be a worldly, wise widow similar to the ones who enjoyed a unique freedom in sophisticated places such as Brighton or London once their spouses were gone (even stashed deep in the country, she'd heard stories aplenty), but Juliet was determined to maintain her independence far away from her restrictive, remaining parent.

"We're down to the last two Mr. Hastings scheduled." Making her way to the back corner after restoring her dress to rights, Oliva, known affectionately as Wivy, edged past the cumbersome partition and glared down at Juliet. "Are you certain I cannot persuade you to halt this mad scheme? Did applicant twenty-three not illustrate the idiocy in continuing?"

"You mean *failure* twenty-three?" Juliet couldn't stop the shudder that convulsed her shoulders. "Wretched man. Taking his irritation with me out on you. We're well rid of that one, I vow."

The bounder! Exasperated with questions Wivy required answers to on Juliet's behalf and enraged at not being graced with her ladyship's presence immediately upon his arrival, he'd had the effrontery to snag Wivy's sleeve and jerk her toward him, his fist raised!

At the horrendous action Juliet could easily observe through the screen they'd worked to strategically place so she could see through it, though the men were "kept in the dark" about her presence, she had burst clumsily from her concealed corner, brandishing her homemade crutch. Her burly footman Jacks had done the same, charging in from his preferred position just outside the door—minus the crutch. Jacks didn't need such props to instill fear, his formidable size being more than sufficient for the challenge.

Now that both men were gone, Juliet couldn't help but ask herself: *Was* she totally addled to continue believing such a bird-witted plan held the answer? Entrusting the fates of herself and all those relying on her on the outcome of one lone, beetle-headed advertisement?

Pushing past Wivy with a confidence she was far from feeling, Juliet stretched her legs, with some measure of difficulty, across the expanse of her sitting room. Brought up to breed an heir and little else (proficiency at French, watercolors and selecting complementary lengths of yarn for embroidery projects notwithstanding), Juliet had neither the training nor the knowledge to return her late husband's exhaustive grounds back to their former glory. Not without funds or a strong man at her side. It seemed creditors and, sadly, her own tenants distrusted even the most heartfelt of assurances and expressively disliked following instructions from a woman when there wasn't a man behind her to back them up.

She and the few servants who remained had outrun the most persistent creditors, retreating first to one neglected property then another until landing here: the most dismal home she now had the misfortune to own, where half the windows were boarded over to avoid the dreaded window tax. More importantly, where she hoped to conduct her interviews with a modicum of peace.

Peace? Hah!

There'd been little enough of that because time grew ever shorter, the portions on their plates ever smaller, and the leaks overhead, as the second bucket brought into her bedchamber could attest, ever larger. A far-off rumble of thunder punctuated her thoughts.

"We're doing the right thing, depend upon it." The only thing, given how she refused to put herself at the mercy of another *titled* gent ever again. If she dragged her feet, um *foot*, much longer in this regard, her overbearing father was sure to arrive on her doorstep with preacher and picked-out pompous peer in tow. And that would never do.

"No..." She slowed her thumped pacing and returned to her place as Wivy again arranged the elaborate divider, masking her presence. "The men answering my advertisement are desperate in their own right. They wouldn't face wedding a complete unknown otherwise." There'd been third and fourth sons, a military man or two and several accomplished tradesmen in their ranks. But there hadn't been a single one she'd remotely considered choosing —not yet. "If neither of these last men come up to snuff, I'll have Mr. Hastings start scheduling another batch of interviews. Fear not. It's simply our job to weed through the chaff and discover the toff most likely to nurture the grounds until they again bloom and prosper."

There now, Juliet congratulated herself. She'd sounded appropriately certain. But after the unexpected setback stemming from last week's Injurious Mishap (though Wivy claimed it was more along the lines of a Canine Catastrophe) and her inability to find a suitable candidate by now, Juliet dreaded, deep inside, that she might have set herself on a losing course. "It's been a long several days, I know, but let us see this through." *For I know not what else to do.* "Only two more. Did you not say so yourself?"

Pray God, one of them was her future husband.

Jacks poked his head in the doorway. “That bleedin’ mort didn’t leave any lasting marks, did ’e?”

“Bleed*ing*?” Wivy asked, her voice rising.

Through the crewel-worked screen, Juliet saw Jacks’ smile widen. “’E is now.”

One could take a boxer from the ring, Juliet mused, biting her lip against a reluctant grin, but couldn’t take the fight out of him. She might not have many servants left, but the ones who’d remained were unfailingly loyal. “We’re both in a fine twig,” she called out, “owing to your swift intervention. My sincere appreciation! Now, do please send in our next man.”

“Before ’Enry can lick ’is ear,” Jacks promised, smacking one fist into the opposite palm. “And you can bet I’ll be right outside the door like always. Just in case another tries getting orn’ry.”

“Speaking of Henry,” Juliet wondered out loud, “where’s he off to?” She hadn’t seen tail nor whisker of her beloved tomcat all day.

“Like as not,” Wivy answered with asperity, “he decamped upstairs to the bedchambers once today's applicants started arriving. That or the kitchen. And who can blame him, after last week's Currish Calamity?"

There was that. Juliet's leg twinged in sympathy.

Attempting to arrange her skirts around the wooden chair that took up most of the cramped space, she looked beyond the embroidered scene that hid her presence. In front of her but angled so Juliet could see the room, Wivy situated herself at the desk.

"Ready to have another go?" Juliet whispered.

Wivy took a deep breath and released it on a loud sigh. "Two more," Juliet heard her murmur. "Two more, then the blessed respite of the weekend."

Juliet knew this marriage scheme had been hard on her friend. For years, she'd been the one constant in Juliet's life. If it weren't for Wivy's companionship, Juliet's betrothal to Lord Letheridge at sixteen—with Papa refusing to grant her the opportunity of a season, much less the chance to meet any other gentlemen—might've been her undoing.

As it was, by the time their extended engagement elapsed and the pompous ceremony held at St. George's as her dear mama insisted (her mother's dying wish, else Juliet had no doubt Papa would've disregarded it as he had all her others), old Leth's determination had dwindled, his winkle had waned, and though Juliet couldn't bring herself to in any way welcome his persistent attempts at bedding her, she'd tolerated them in good stead as she'd been taught a dutiful wife ought.

Yet she remained untouched, in the extreme intimate sense, to this day. Hence, part of her unfailing resolve to have a say in her next spouse. And bed partner.

After all, other young ladies were allowed to choose, didn't have an odious father who gave them no voice, no—

Oh, holy day!

Every righteous thought flew from her brain as she caught sight of a most compelling man hesitating in the doorway. Why did he wait? Why did this one persist in stalling? In not coming closer where she could secure a better look?

Why did her heart jump in her chest and the air in her lungs evaporate to nothing—at nothing more than her first hazy glimpse of him?

Juliet caught herself listing forward and hastily scooted back upon the chair (falling face-first into the screen would certainly *not* aid her cause!). Once firmly situated, she again stared toward the newcomer. Yet he still hadn't moved. Why—

But then he did and she could breathe again, her chest expanding and eyes flaring wide as he passed through the doorway. His former dithering aside, he now stalked purposefully into her sitting room, inspecting his surroundings as if he already owned the space—and everything, every*one* in it.

An unruly shock of dark blond hair fell forward over his forehead, nearly to his jaw. He raked it back, giving her a view of strong, harsh features and brooding eyes, their color indistinguishable from this distance.

Though his size was akin to Jacks', this man moved with an innate, confident grace, his strides long, his Hessians clipping brusquely upon the floor until he gained the rug and stopped, tilting his fair head in deference to Wivy. “Madam.”

He flashed a grin and something dormant inside Juliet flared to life, leaving her feeling bold and anxious and giddy all at once. *Is he the one?*

Regardless of how very serious the entire undertaking was to her future, Juliet couldn’t refrain from gawking at his…um…masculine form. His impressive, muscular thighs specifically.

An audible gasp wound its way up her throat. Juliet clamped one hand over her lips.

A lady wasn’t supposed to acknowledge, even mentally, that a man’s limbs existed, much less *name* them. *Thighs*, she thought again because she could, smiling behind her fingers. Because never again would she let any man rule over her mind or her tongue.

Thighs. Legs.

Simply acknowledging how his drew her made her blood flow hot and thick.

Legs! She wanted to shout it out the open window. *This stranger possesses the most magnificent legs.* Oh, she was brazen indeed!

Lady or not, there was no denying she admired everything outwardly about him—his shaggy hair and craggy face, his legs, hips, waist... thighs, they all fascinated and beckoned.

She swallowed back another gasp, one of pure unadulterated relief. For here was a man worth gasping over, a man worth abandoning maidenly scruples drummed into one from infanthood. A man to inspire all manner of explicit, illicit dreams.

The cumbersome screen now had a new purpose, Juliet realized, lowering her hand and wiping surprisingly damp palms on the layers of skirt and petticoat gathered in her lap: that of allowing her to look her fill, to stare at and ogle this manly specimen in a way no maiden would ever be permitted.

To hope...

Maybe, just maybe, applicant twenty-four would prove to be *the* one.

THE CONDITION of the room appalled Zeus; it matched that of the whole abysmal house, at least the few ghastly portions he'd been privy to. Two blinks away from decrepitude, it somehow seemed wrong to be meeting the infamous Lady Scandal in such a desolate atmosphere. Agonizingly wrong, given how he'd anticipated their meeting occurring at Amherst and not this rachitic ruin.

And after what he'd just seen her footman do, the prior candidate's shouts of outrage at being manhandled by a manservant sufficient inducement to lure both Zeus and the lone remaining applicant into the hallway for the show, Zeus wasn't so sure he *wanted* his turn in these unsavory surroundings. Wasn't so sure his relinquished hat would be spared mangling from the beefy hands he'd just witnessed trouncing the foul-mouthed sod who'd gone directly before him—and who'd just been swiftly evicted from the premises.

Zeus glanced again into the room he was expected to enter, so dingy and pathetic he suspected even moths and mice would pass it by.

Remember why you're here. What she can give you.

Prompted, as always, by the overwhelming goal that continued to guide his every action, even now, years and lifetimes later, Zeus nodded his thanks toward the burly fellow who, after wiping blood and "bad spirits" off his hands and person, had deferentially escorted Zeus through the gloomy maze.

A fortifying breath and Zeus stepped over the threshold. For good or ill, he was committed to his course.

And ill it just might be, given the way his nose prickled at the sour hint of stale smoke that hung in the air. But unlike the crypt of a study he'd been stashed in all day, along with other expectant contenders, where he'd forbore puffing tobacco or drumming fingertips—and outwardly expressing his anxiety—this particular room, upon closer inspection he was delighted to note, exhibited several rays of sunshine to brighten its dreary reality.

Rays of sunshine that proved a balm to his weary soul. A number of them streamed in from the unboarded windows facing west, several splashed about in the form of wild-cut flowers bunched in disreputable vases, and one presided regally before him, her dress every bit as yellow and sunny as the sporadic unfaded rectangles on the walls, bright patches of paper and plaster, loudly proclaiming the paintings she'd been forced to sell off.

She. Lady Scandal, sitting patiently behind her desk, a look of wary resignation on her face.

One glance put him in mind of a fetchingly plump and eminently beddable tavern wench. The kind he'd feasted on in his youth, the kind he'd avoided of late. The anti-lady.

Over the last weeks, he'd built Lady Scandal up in his mind as a genteel, dainty creature, desperate enough for funds to overlook his disreputable birth. Though his blighted beginnings certainly matched the state of her home, the regal daffodil looked anything but desperate.

Although appealing in an earthy, buxom way, she was not what Zeus had primed himself for, and he couldn't stop the dual pings of disappointment—that she didn't resemble the elegant "lady" his deuced imaginings had conjured, and that he wasn't attracted to her as he ought to be his *wife*, the one woman he'd forsake all others on behalf of until death did they part.

His primed poker wilted a bit, expressing its dismay. In opposition, Zeus stiffened his legs, and shoved any dirk disappointment aside. He wasn't here for *her*, he reminded himself; he was here for what he could get *from* her.

"Madam." He proffered a perfunctory bow. "Z. J. Tanner, at your service. I believe we have much to discuss, you and I."

She smiled at him, a true welcome meant to put him at ease, and another brilliant beam of sunshine graced the tired room.

Unexpectedly, his heart went out to her, this brave woman willing to sacrifice all to rebuild her surroundings, and if no other part of his anatomy made its empathy or potential excitement known, well...Zeus determinedly stamped down any discontent. *Brains over ballocks*, he mentally prompted, repeating the refrain that'd become his constant companion and bedfellow of late.

After making his introduction, he allowed his gaze to journey once more around the spacious room. Behind the daffodil—the future Mrs. Tanner?—an intricately embroidered screen occupied the corner. The magnum opus looked woefully out of place, more suited to a museum than this mausoleum.

An unlit, crumbling fireplace commanded the opposite wall. A simple settee, low table before it, laden with two of the fragrant bouquets, and a couple of rigid-looking, worn parlor chairs filled the rug where he'd halted.

She gestured toward the ugly chairs. "Please sit, Mr. Tanner. I'll endeavor to make this as painless as possible."

"I'd prefer to stand, if that's agreeable."

"By all means." She smiled again, the cheerful expression lessening the sense of doom he'd refused to acknowledge since seeing a number of other like-minded dolts summoned and summarily discarded before him, until it was down to him and one other. Though the remaining man, a former seafaring one, appeared a good sort, Zeus was determined to win the lady—and her accompanying bounty.

When she cordially explained, "I am Olivia Hales, my lady's companion. She has entrusted me with the task of ascertaining your responses to several questions," Zeus' fading apprehension roared back to the surface, intensified beyond measure.

How many more mountains must he climb before meeting "my lady"?

First obtaining the plethora of character references, then enduring the punctilious Hastings, who insisted on reading them all save the one from his former mistress—thank God for small favors—and now this...being vetted by a servant. Ah, well. If it meant gaining Amherst, he could withstand anything, Zeus told himself, blowing out his frustration on a hearty sigh.

At the sound of his impatience, the daffodil raised one eyebrow.

"I'd initially taken you for her ladyship," Zeus confessed, widening his stance since it appeared he'd be here awhile. He locked his hands behind him, determined not to display any further unease.

"You did?" If possible, that brightened her smile. "My lady regrets she was called away. She'll join us as soon as she's able."

"I admit to being more than a trifle disappointed that I now must again postpone making the acquaintance of such an obviously admired woman."

"Pardon?"

"Both you and Hastings appear to be troubling yourselves extensively to aid in her...shall we say...*quest* for a savior."

"She seeks a spouse," the companion chided, "not someone sent from the Almighty."

Zeus allowed his gaze to pointedly fix upon the tattered upholstery seat of one chair. "She seeks someone to save her from the poorhouse and her posterior from ill-padded cushions."

He thought he heard a snicker, but it was quickly muffled behind her hand. "Yes...well, be that as it may, shall we proceed?"

"I am at your disposal." As long as you do not dispose of my suit.

"What prompted you to respond to my lady's advertisement?"

"The inducements stated therein."

"Are you overly fond of dogs?"

"Not excessively, no." Not since a vile one chased him, instilling terror in a five-year-old's heart.

"Would you have any aversion to your wife spending her pin money on fripperies?"

"Fripperies?" Was he about to shackle himself to some gadfly spendthrift? One who'll have no respect for the chink he spent years acquiring? "Can you please expound upon what might constitute a frippery in her mind?"

"Oh, you know, simply things of nonsense... hair ribbons. Yarn."

Ribbons...yarn? Neither of which amounted to the vast sums he'd feared at the question. "None whatsoever."

"Please share your thoughts on the education of children."

That was unexpected. Dogs, yarn... Hell, most all these deuced questions were unexpected. Regretting that he'd allowed the monstrous servant to relieve him of gloves and hat, Zeus flexed his empty hands. He knotted them in place at the base of his spine. "Education for the wee ones? I...I confess to never giving that topic lengthy consideration."

"Please do so now, if you would."

"Ah...children. They need some manner of learning to gain a foothold in this world, to keep them from starving in the streets. Book learning might do well for some, but trades are good too."

She seemed to hesitate and he caught a slight rustle behind her. Then she straightened. "What about girls?"

"Girls? What about them?"

"Should they be allowed to learn?"

"I don't see why not." He thought of his mother and her lack of options once being used and discarded. "Otherwise they're dependent upon the whims of men."

"You are to be commended, Mr. Tanner."

He was? "I am?"

"You're very progressive in your thinking."

Avoiding the look of surprise in her gaze, Zeus shifted his. "Suppose that makes up for all my regressive living."

He'd meant it as a jest. Didn't seem funny once voiced. Zeus rolled his shoulders, hoping the tenseness with which he held himself didn't show. Wondering how much longer he'd have to wait to greet Lady Scandal. Just the name conjured sweaty bodies and entangled limbs. Delivering hot, wet kisses over the pale skin of her throat, the small of her back. Running his tongue down the arch of a dainty foot while said lady sprawled nude before him, basking in the decadent attention, her impassioned moans begging him to bring his staff closer to her waiting lips.

Zeus licked his, ready to savor her scandalous taste, bask in her flavor, in the fragrant aroma he just knew would be exuding from her—

"Have you any experience successfully managing estates?"

The question came from far off, miles from the darkened bedchamber invading his mind.

"Mr. Tanner." The daffodil recalled him to the room, the ugly, anything-but-succulent room, and asked again, "Have you any experience successfully managing estates?"

Estates. Now this was more in line with what he'd expected. *Amherst over amour*, he reminded his wayward-thinking mind and answered truthfully. "None at all."

Keeping his attention firmly entrenched in *this* room, he allowed his gaze to be drawn behind her, to the crewel work decorating the framed partition. The outdoor scene was magnificently rendered.

"You've experience, then, managing them *unsuccessfully*?"

"No, not that either." He turned to face her, catching sight of a forlorn expression. "No experience overseeing estates at all."

"Yet you wish to do so now?"

"With all my heart."

"Are you so very confident of your success, then? At so new an endeavor?"

"I cannot claim it with absolute certainty when so many facets beyond my influence come into play, Mother Nature being but one. It is a vast undertaking we discuss, of that I'm aware, but I vow to give it my unceasing effort." Again his gaze fell on the screen's outdoor scene. Shade trees, a waterfall, intricate vines of flowers adorning the perimeter...all created with *yarn*.

"What are the biggest failings you declare?"

"My failings?" His brows rose and he left off inspecting the impressive landscape to turn his attention to what—or who—might lie beyond it. "Would you not rather have an accounting of my successes? Estate management aside, I've had a number—"

"Let me articulate it differently. What are your most significantly unpleasant character traits? Deficiencies in your personality a wife might need to contend with?"

Personality deficiencies? These questions were enough to make his stomach roil!

After leaving Duffield at first light and traveling the seventeen miles on horseback to this neglected property where Hastings insisted he report—and not Amherst as he'd anticipated—then cooling his heels for hours in the grim study while studying his competition, Zeus realized hunger was likely the culprit his innards felt walloped, but regardless, he simply wanted to be done with these infernal questions. Wanted to meet the real Lady Scandal in the flesh, evaluate how eager his flesh was to join with hers.

Ready to bear his children, indeed. Vexing woman wouldn't even bare her face. "I'm an absolute *bear* when hungry," he fairly growled.

How much longer would he be obliged to wait? First the interminable delay in Duffield where Hastings had somehow scrounged the ballocks to order Zeus not to venture past the village. In defiance, he'd set out for Amherst three times, only to have ferocious storms boil up from nothing, forcing him back. As if Fate didn't want him catching a glimpse of his long-denied reward.

"Very prettily answered. Now please tell me something less cavalier."

He ordered his hands to stop strangling each other and brought his mangled fingers in front of him, clapping his palms together. "I'm impatient. I tend to be unforgiving when wronged. I don't suffer fools, and in my experience, most all aristocrats act foolish. I—"

"'Tis enough, I'm sure." She held up one gloved hand, biting back another smile if he wasn't mistaken. "Can we then assume you aren't a thief nor a murderer?"

"We?" His eyes flicked toward the partition behind her. *Lady Scandal, my patience is hanging by a thread...*

"You and I," the companion replied, plumping her cheeks by freeing another of those cheerful smiles.

"A murderer? Nay. But I have been a thief."

"Uh-ahhh..." She seemed at a loss, choking on some sort of reply.

Well, good. Strangest accounting of questions he'd ever been a party to. Most frustrating as well.

Zeus caught the hint of a whisper, then the daffodil cocked her ear toward the corner. So there *was* someone back there.

It irked him that these "ladies" were playing games with his life. "Why don't you show yourself?" he called out, overloud. "Face your future husband and pelter him with questions directly?"

Let me see whether you live up to your name? And my infernal imaginings.

2

AN EXCHANGE OF FORFEITS GOES AFOOT (ER, AWRY)

"In due time," the mysterious female rejoined immediately.

For not demurring, reluctant esteem for the woman rose in Zeus, though he couldn't resist tapping one booted foot on the floor. When the edge of the rug that'd seen better years muffled the sound, he shifted back a step and tapped again. Louder.

"Exhibiting your lack of patience won't hasten the process, I can assure you," the same dulcet, unattributed voice admonished.

Plowing one hand through his hair, Zeus commanded his feet to still.

Displaying the composure he *wished* he felt, the companion calmly turned back to him. "Would you care to elaborate upon the circumstances which caused you to steal?"

"No, I would not."

"Would you tell us anyway?" His mysterious wife-to-be asked through the screen.

Damn female, making it sound as though she uttered a sweetly phrased request when they both knew it was one he dare not ignore. He might hold the purse in this potential partnership, but she held all the strings. At least for now.

"Mr. Tanner?" his nebulous nemesis prompted.

"My mother was unwell," he shared reluctantly.

It was a time he preferred not to dwell on or speak of, but when that brought no response from either of them, Zeus felt obliged to elucidate. "It was a harsh winter. She'd fallen ill and could no longer work. She was starving."

"And you?" came the disembodied voice, subdued now. "Were you hungry as well?"

Zeus didn't attempt to stifle his small but very real smile. "That I was, but my thieving had an unexpected boon when the butcher caught me pilfering his bacon."

He heard a relieved sigh from the unseen woman. "Made you his apprentice, did he?"

"Nay, but he did make my mum his wife."

"You may proceed to the next question, Wivy."

"Why don't you ask it yourself, madam?" His own impertinence surprised him, given all that was at stake, but he forged ahead nevertheless. "It is with understandable urgency that I desire to make your acquaintance through something other than an embroidered barrier or the indomitable Hastings."

"Soon enough, my impatient applicant," she said with an indulgent smile in her voice. "Do carry on, Wivy."

The blonde grinned at him, and if Zeus didn't know any better, he'd think she gave him an encouraging nod, indicating he was doing well.

"Please tell us about your strengths—and before you ask, I don't mean how many stone you can lift or carry but your personality strengths, those that comprise your moral fiber."

From the hidden corner, a rusty cackle of what he thought passed for laughter jolted through him, chasing the shadows from his memories. "I think we can glean that one ourselves, Wivy!"

"Madam?" He turned to face his invisible adversary and bowed his head in a show of respect before yanking it upright and glaring at that damnable shield. No doubt, she could see him while obscuring herself. "What character strength do you believe you've already ascertained and on such short acquaintance?" And by God, what the deuce was he doing bantering with her? This virago who hid herself and ordered others to do her bidding, likely so ugly or so old she feared running off suitors at first glance. But no...that oddly enchanting, uninhibited cackle of a laugh couldn't belong to a crone. Or could it?

In return, the chosen applicant will receive a genteel, amiable wife ready to bear his children. Female in question is of sound intellect and generally appealing countenance, he recalled, hoping to mitigate his growing concerns. Appealing countenance, heh? He'd like to see for himself.

"*Honesty*, Mr. Tanner. Based on your pithy replies, it is quite apparent you possess forthright honesty." Before he could react to that pronouncement, she continued. "Please tell us about *your* education."

"It came from the streets of London. Back alleys too."

"Then you know *nothing* of estate management?" She sounded vastly disappointed.

"I wasn't asked about my education in the realm of estate management, now was I? Only of my experience."

"I'm asking now."

"Last I checked, the streets of London contained lending libraries. While my practical application of such knowledge may be nominal..." He placed the tips of two fingers to the side of his head and rapped lightly. "The information is here, I promise you, simply waiting for the opportunity to be utilized." Zeus started to rattle off a number of facts about Amherst and the vast lands comprising it but decided demonstrating his extensive knowledge of crops and herds, of tenants and taxes could wait until *he* garnered some answers. "I'd like to begin asking a few questions of my own, starting with how the blazes a female who lacks the gumption to show her face expects to convince me of her 'readiness to bear my children'? That is part of the bargain, as I recall, and unless you intend to practice immaculate conception right along with the Blessed Virgin, you'll be showing me significantly more than your face before the deed is done!"

"Mr. Tanner!" The daffodil's cheeks flamed. Her hands fluttered. "I— I..."

He felt rotten. Mum had taught him better. "Forgive me. I didn't mean to render you speechless nor take my *honest impatience* out on anyone."

A muffled snort, then another splurt of hilarity met his ears. "Wivy, you may leave now. I'll conduct the rest of the interview." The embroidered scene trembled, followed by yet another snort. "I do believe I'd like to be alone with our guest."

Satisfaction surged through Zeus. Now he and the mysterious Lady Scandal would get somewhere. Somewhere that led him closer to her body, and closer to Amherst. Although, at the moment, he was more eager to meet the "lady" who possessed such unladylike laughter —laughter he somehow found eminently engaging—than he was to seek redress for ancient acts of contempt and derision. Trifling now, they almost seemed, when he was faced with his *future.*

Though since meeting her—or nearly so—his conscience nagged, poking at him like a pointy pebble in his boot. *Tell her the truth. All of it.* Ignoring the annoying sense of scruples, Zeus rammed his hair back, wishing he could see through the partition as easily.

AS SHE ADMIRED the slightly muddled specimen of male perfection through the tightly woven threads of the divider, Juliet had to remember she was invisible to him. One wouldn't know it, the way he fixed his gaze upon her precise location, fairly stripping her bare with the fierce expression he directed her way.

An evocative warmth spiraled through her in the wake of his heated gaze, tensing her muscles and setting her on edge. Flickering about her stomach and bringing a boldness to her tongue she'd not employed before, not with a father and then a husband who each maintained womenfolk should be blindly—and silently—obedient in all things.

Feminine opinions were *not* to be voiced. Certainly not heard and considered.

But from the way Mr. Tanner held himself and beheld her through the screen, all confident cockiness and self assurance in spite of the outrageous answers he supplied, Juliet doubted he'd allow himself to be threatened by any "mere" woman.

In fact, part of her dared speculate...might he *solicit* her opinions on occasion, given how, even though he made his reluctance keenly apparent, he remained amenable to discussing each and every query topic she broached? A husband who talked with her! Would that not be sparkish fine?

And Lord how her throat hurt! He made her laugh, this particular applicant. Causing the rusty, seldom-used reflex to scrape up her neck and emerge without constraint, sounding somewhat like a braying donkey she feared, but oh, how wonderful it felt. Almost as wonderful as the wicked, wanton urges he brought forth with nothing but his presence.

Juliet's fingers ached to touch the strong, corded muscles of his neck visible above his simply tied cravat, the muscles that even now worked as he clenched his jaw. No surprise, given the subterfuge he'd caught her enacting. But unlike the previous man who'd turned nasty when he'd found her out, Mr. Tanner only challenged her to face him, to *speak* with him.

"Please, Wivy," she whispered, not above pleading with her friend to leave them alone, but not wanting him to hear how desperately. After the plethora of unsuccessful interviews they'd conducted the last couple of weeks, after all she'd endured, she'd truly begun to despair of ever finding a potential, decent mate.

It was a miracle she hadn't canceled the entire scheme. While she'd seriously contemplated abandoning everything a time or two during some of the more wretched interviews, she hadn't.

And now a man stood before her, his responses nearly so absurdly perfect, Juliet was half afraid to ask him anything else. But ask she must.

Others were dependent upon her.

Even though her melting insides craved for him to be the one, she couldn't hide from the reality that his last response didn't bode well. His lack of estate management experience should've been the red flag that waved him on his way. But she couldn't turn loose, not yet. Not of him, nor of her hopes.

Because on so many levels, Mr. Tanner seemed *exactly* right. Time and again, his at turns baffling and belligerent responses proved he was the first candidate to appeal to her in all areas she'd set forth:

~ cordiality to Wivy and Jacks (An indication, she believed, of how he might treat tenants, children…and a wife.);

~ integrity and candor (She allowed his responses up to this point indicated both. If they also indicated an unwillingness to be led by a ring through his nose, all the better. She needed a man who wasn't afraid to stand up to those who *thought* they were better than everyone else.);

~ a willingness to educate females (He'd managed to supply this perfect response without once smirking, earning her undying devotion early on.);

~ a disinclination to pander to whining whelps (She'd added this requirement just last week.);

~ interest and knowledge of estate matters (Grasping at straws, she reasoned Mr. Tanner's inexperience in this area was offset by his abundance of honesty.);

~ and *not* most important of all, her mind insisted, but as though staging a mutiny, her body persisted upon disagreeing, it was paramount she found him attractive. Visually riveting. (Which she most assuredly did!).

If Juliet was to barter her future by willingly shackling herself to another man, then, sure as tits trilled and cocks crowed, she wanted to *want* him. With everything in her.

The low, constant pressure building deep in her abdomen and flittering about her chest told her she wanted Mr. Tanner.

At least clothed, she did.

And that gave her pause. Attired, despite his advanced years, Lord Letheridge had cut a tolerable figure. But once the padded jacket was removed, the contoured stockings peeled away, and his sunken chest and pasty skin revealed, his bare form had repulsed her every bit as much as his repugnant personality.

Therefore, Juliet had two vital qualities to ascertain before deciding whether Mr. Tanner was the spouse she sought: how he appeared *unclothed* and how he conducted himself as a lover.

The idea of Mr. Tanner, naked and acting the lover *toward* her? It was more than enough for

Juliet to discard all pretense of decorum and steer the interview in the naughty direction she hoped it might take. She swallowed past the knot of nervous excitement the torrid thought brought forth.

"Wivy, you must leave," she demanded as quietly as she dared. "*Please heed me on this.*" Then louder, "Olivia, do please tell the remaining gentleman how very appreciative I am he expended himself to such a degree but that I won't be able to see him today." Poor fellow, she really should compensate him for his time, but funds were so very low. Cook did make a thumping good scone however. (When they weren't out of sugar, that was.) "I'm afraid I can't reimburse his travel expenses, but if you would see he's served refreshments before he leaves?

"Oh!" Goodness, she'd nearly forgotten her other area of evaluation, not having many occasions to administer it. "And tell Jacks he may bring in the refreshment tray at his convenience."

Wivy shot her an inscrutable look and muttered, "I like this one but I certainly hope you know what you're doing." Then she quit the room, skirting around Mr. Tanner but only *after* imparting something to him Juliet couldn't make out.

Hmm. Now what was Wivy about? No matter. Juliet had just gained her goal: time alone with applicant twenty-four. A hitch to her breathing told her she hadn't been this excited in years.

Juliet smiled. But then she frowned. Her lower half was decidedly uncomfortable. She shifted on her hard chair, attempted to cross her legs—to squeeze out the lingering ache that'd settled there—to no avail. The ache persisted. "Well, now…it's just me and you, Mr. Tanner." She shifted again and tried not to sound so out of breath. "Shall we continue?"

He brought one well-muscled leg forward, then stopped. "Not until you tell me how I fare. Talking to an invisible Lady Scandal—"

"Lady Scandal? That's what they're calling me?" Of a certainty, *scandalous* fit how she felt, staring waist-high at his flexing thighs and…um, *things* centered above and between.

"Aye, but at being denied your actual acquaintance, I'm feeling the bamboozled dupe, thinking I'm here on a sleeveless errand and nothing more."

When he looked back toward the door, as if contemplating escape, Juliet stammered, "Nay! I'm not trifling with you! To be sure, I find you intrepid and impudent and a host of other things I'm too much a lady to mention."

"That bad, eh?"

"That good, I fear."

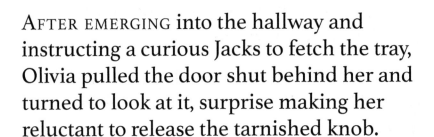

AFTER EMERGING into the hallway and instructing a curious Jacks to fetch the tray, Olivia pulled the door shut behind her and turned to look at it, surprise making her reluctant to release the tarnished knob.

Well. That had been unexpected. Leave her charge and bosom friend alone with a truthful thief? And a formidable, scowling specimen to boot.

Peeling paint marked the stout door she hesitated to move from, the chipped antique white antiqued more by time than design. After it had collapsed off its hinges their first week in residence, Jacks and their remaining stable boy (who needed more than one when they no longer had any horseflesh that required stabling?) had rehung it to its current non-listing exactness.

The exchange of indistinct murmurs reached her from the depths of the sitting room, one deep and just a shade from belligerent. The other carefree. Joyous almost.

Recalling his sincere look, and the quickly masked vulnerability if she wasn't mistaken, in Mr. Tanner's gaze just before she acquiesced and quit the room convinced Olivia that Juliet was in no danger. Unlike that lout they'd interviewed just prior, the one who'd exhibited no ability to laugh at anything, much less at himself, she sensed Mr. Tanner possessed enough self-assurance and inherent composure that nothing unduly untoward would occur.

Pah. Applicant twenty-three. To resort to violence and all because the ruffian took exception to being "duped by two bitches" or so he'd claimed when Juliet had the misfortune to sneeze, giving them both away. Crude churl! Thinking he could buy his way into respectability, as though money answered everything. Give her a man with a ready smile and a good appreciation of the absurd, a hard worker not afraid to get his hands dirty and able to laugh in the process. She'd take that over one with sovereigns to spare any day.

Actually most days of late, Olivia would be grateful if only a man would look at her and really see her. It'd been a long, long time since a fellow had aimed attention her direction with something akin to interest lighting his eyes. Companions were paid (or not paid, in her particular case) to blend into the background. To become invisible. Something she'd perhaps accomplished with too much zeal?

She thought of the way Mr. Tanner had gazed at the screen. With hope. And determination.

And that was before he'd ever clapped his peepers on the fair Lady Juliet. Aye, her mistress was in good hands at the moment. Safe, strong hands, if she didn't miss her guess, and Olivia had always considered herself a fair judge of character.

With a decisive nod, she steeled her resolve and abandoned her station. Duty called.

Tell the final applicant he wasn't needed? It was a task she dreaded. To be cast last and now discarded without an audience? What man would take kindly to such news?

"Oh, bother it, Wivy!" Unconsciously, she used Juliet's pet name. Perhaps in an attempt to shore up her own shaky confidence? Lord knew sweet Juliet didn't lack in the courage department.

Determined to see the onerous task over and quickly, Olivia swept down the long hallway, cringing when a bit of wall plaster dusted her dress when Jacks approached, his arms laden with refreshments, and she stepped aside.

"This bodes well, do ye think?" Jacks halted to ask.

"What? That she wanted to be alone with Mr. Tanner? Aye, I do. Tell me, Jacks, is our remaining guest still situated in the study?"

Jacks gave a brief shake of his head. "Asked if 'e could stretch 'is legs a bit when I came for the Tanner gent. Believe 'e's out back, walkin' the garden fer a spell."

"Very well. Carry on."

"You'll see to 'im then?"

See him off, he meant? "That I will."

Olivia proceeded toward the stairs, thinking, and not for the first time, how this old, neglected home could shine if only someone would devote some tender love and thoughtful care to it. *Much like yourself?*

And where had that come from? Juliet was the one who'd instigated the Marriage Scheme. Olivia just wanted the whole ordeal over and her friend happily settled.

At least, that's what she continually told herself. On-the-shelf companions weren't considered marriage material. Far from it. And the sooner she quit contemplating otherwise, the more content she'd likely be.

Upon reaching the landing, she mentally chanted *three, eleven* and *seventeen*. Three, eleven, seventeen. Those were the ricketiest treads, the ones they all took pains to avoid. Beneath the board nailed over it, tread four had a boot-sized hole gouged in the baluster side, compliments of Jacks the day upon their arrival.

But the flocked amaranthus paper lining the opposite wall had an aged grace Olivia found charming. Truth be told, despite its sadly neglected air and propensity toward rot (thanks, she was sure, to the splintered roof tiles and resulting leaks) Olivia found the old house charming.

Especially the gardens.

Not nearly as overgrown as one might expect given the state of the structure they surrounded, the grounds still retained a glimmer of their former sparkle. Safely bypassing the last questionable stair, Olivia sidestepped a chipped tile in the entry and headed for the massive front door, wrenching it open after only two attempts. Better at weather predictions than any soothsayer or trick knee, the wood always swelled when rain approached.

The verdant, lush green of a spring in full bloom greeted her, lent a lift to her spirits, and Olivia fairly skipped over the flagstone path that circled the old manor. She was intent on intercepting their errant applicant before he came back inside. Bad news was best broken under a sunny sky, or so her mama had always claimed. Olivia spared a quick glance upward and decided a cloudy sky would have to do.

Rounding the second corner, her feet came to an abrupt halt. Her breath hissed inward. Her eyes nearly bugged to Bedfordshire and back.

And her heart? That hurly-burly organ took off like a galloping horse—stealing away with her common sense perhaps?

Because, instead of swooning or shying away, instead of yelling loudly for Jacks, Olivia stood, happily, *hungrily* in place. She stood stock-still and she stared at the sumptuous sight, watching the play of muscle across a strong, bare back as applicant twenty-five (for who else could it be?), completely unaware of her presence, wielded a Dutch hoe in one corner of the weed-infested herb garden. But most notable of all? He was dressed in nothing more than black tall boots and tight black breeches.

Obscenely tight breeches.

Well now. And to think, Juliet had complained there wasn't anything of value remaining on the grounds.

Olivia begged to differ.

Neither did she make a sound to inform him of her presence. She might have been trained to teach proper behavior and exhibit it herself, but she knew enough about life and death, about expectations and disappointments to know opportunity didn't often knock. Especially opportunities for observing and admiring a strong, sweaty man wearing absurdly tight breeches.

So she watched. And her dratted throat betrayed her, making some sort of begging, yearning noise that had her unexpected treat jerking upright and whirling around.

"Oh!" was all he said, a gruff sound of surprise.

Oh was right. Oh great day in the gloomy afternoon, she'd never seen such a handsome man. With his shirt off.

And staring right at her as though he *liked* what he saw.

Her.

Well now. Mayhap this wouldn't be such an onerous task after all.

ZEUS ALLOWED his posture to relax and stepped aside when Lady Juliet's servant brought in a tray laden with sweets and a steaming teapot, the advice—or admonishment, he hadn't quite decided which—delivered by the daffodil on her way out still ringing in his ear: "She possesses more brains than sense, but it comes with a heart of gold. Be gentle with her."

Gentle? What manner of treatment had this cautiously audacious lass been subjected to?

The burly man placed the tray on the table before turning to address the screen. "Milady?"

"That will be all, Jacks, thank you. Close the door and please see that we're not disturbed."

"*Milady?*" The request obviously surprised him. Which pleased Zeus to no end. So she *wasn't* in the habit of secreting herself away with suitors? Realizing he was an exception, a surge of male pride stroked his ego. Made him all the more eager to stroke something of hers. Sultry lips, perhaps? Dainty feet? Everywhere in between?

"Ahem." The man coughed loudly, making no effort to disguise his concern. "Alone, milady? Are you cer—"

"*Quite.* You may relax your vigil, dear Jacks," she insisted, and Zeus fancied he heard a blush in her voice. "*Leave your post.* Enjoy the rest of the day," she all but ordered, "before those encroaching clouds drench out the remaining sunshine." Proving she *could* see him—him and the darkening sky through the window beyond.

The manservant cut his eyes toward Zeus, who gave a confirming nod, appearing more assured than he felt—or so he hoped. "Your lady shall come to no harm on my watch, of that I can promise." It wouldn't harm her if he did away with that pesky partition, now would it?

"Very good, milady." With a diffident nod, and a slight narrowing of his gaze toward Zeus, the man quit the room by way of a reluctant backward walk.

After the door clicked shut, Zeus stood there in the stillness, curiosity—among other things—aroused. "What manner of topics shall I expound upon now? Or are you finally ready to emerge from behind your shield?" *Before I rip it away?*

"Partake of a scone, please," the melodious voice demanded.

"And if I do not care for a scone?" he countered, wanting some say in this deuced lopsided encounter. But also wondering how long she intended to hide and curious how she intended to progress things from here.

She huffed, and he could just see her hands compressed in her lap, knuckles white with frustration. Although any irritation with him was completely absent in her tone when she added, "If you will *please* partake of a scone and a cup of tea, upon their completion I shall explain the reason behind it."

An alarming thought struck him. "They aren't poisoned?"

"You think—?" This time, the muffled snort sounded more like a choked gurgle. "You think, after *inviting* you here, after offering my hand in exchange for your money, I plan to send you out on six men's shoulders?"

His own chuckle rumbled forth. "Put that way, I suppose not."

"Certainly not, I assure you! I hold the men who exert themselves responding to my advertisement in the highest regard, at least until they prove themselves undeserving of said regard. Nevertheless, I would not wish to so precipitously end their existence! Poisoned scones, indeed. Shame, Mr. Tanner, for thinking such."

"No, shame on you for *hiding* once these initially estimable men arrive," he grumbled as he eased onto one of her ugly chairs and tried not to flinch when it creaked. Then creaked again when a massive bundle of marmalade fur jumped onto his lap and sunk its claws into his buckskins.

Zeus ground his teeth against the knifepoints piercing into his leg. "Who have we here?"

"Henry!" she exclaimed in astonished tones. "Mr. Tanner, count yourself among the exclusive minority who have received *his* approval!"

While the cat made mincemeat of his breeches, Zeus brushed one hand over its back and retrieved a scone off a horridly elegant tea service with the other. Hoping to lure her out—so he could take his measure of her exterior—he queried at his most cultured, "Would you not care for one, my lady?"

"Mayhap later. Do eat it now, please, if you would."

Taking care with the fragile pastry, Zeus brought it to his mouth for a sizable bite.

Instead of the warm rush of buttery bliss he expected, a salty chunk of grit met his tongue.

Straining to keep his expression bland, he chewed and chewed again, trying to work up sufficient saliva to swallow the field of dirt dwelling in his mouth. Finally, fearful of choking to death, he coaxed the bite down, placed the remainder on a napkin, and took a sip of hearty tea. Returning the cup to a saucer smaller than his palm, Zeus straightened. "Er...*ack*...delightful."

His thighs had gone numb, which the marmalade monstrosity made up for by standing on his hind legs to butt Zeus' chin with his purring head before jumping down.

"Do you not seek to finish the scone?"

No, he did not. He hacked into his closed fist, then looked up and attempted a game smile. Despite her assurances to the contrary, was she in truth *trying* to kill him? "Would it please you were I to do so?"

Kick the bucket or finish the scone, Zeus was no longer sure what he inquired after.

"Very much so. Complete the scone and tea, and an explanation shall be yours."

"I'd rather have the sight of your face, the taste of your lips," he told the embroidered waterfall, surmising she blushed beyond.

When a small gasp was her only response, Zeus steeled himself, picked up the silt pile, and took a second briny bite. Gnashing past the Sahara, praying again for saliva, he wondered what manner of woman lurked beyond fearsome footmen, stubborn solicitors and dusty dainties?

Was she, too, as dilapidated as her home? As tattered and worn—his eyes drifted to the other chair—as her surroundings?

He braved another swallow, managed not to sputter dust, and shifted upon his uncomfortable perch. Was she as unyielding as her furnishings?

The third bite made its way to his tongue, and as his mind drifted toward pleasant, favorable thoughts, so his salivary glands followed.

Or was she, perhaps, the opposite of everything around her? Impeccable, immaculate, and... yielding? As soft and welcoming as her prickly, affectionate cat? As ready to sit upon his lap?

The next bite went down easier. He opened wide for the remainder, ready to finish the task for the reward she'd promised.

Would her taste beguile him, as did her peculiar laugh? More raspy rooster than girlish giggle, the sound wound through every lonely, belligerent corner of his soul each time he heard it, infusing the dark, scorned patches with light...and hope.

Damn, he wanted to see her, touch her. Taste her.

As if he lived for parched, salt-dunked scones, Zeus swallowed and smiled, his lips anticipating their first taste of the lady and the laughter behind the curtain. After a cursory brush with a napkin, he held up empty hands.

“Bravo! I am delighted!” She applauded.

He reached for the remaining tea. “That I ate a,” *sorry-arse*, “scone without choking?”

“That you did so without spewing crumbs nor spittle down your shirtfront!”

Tea abandoned, he gained his feet. “*That* was the test? What manner of barbarian do you take me for?”

“Not you, Mr. Tanner, never you.” The assurance didn’t mollify him until he heard the sigh of relief she expelled. Damn. Ole Lecherous had been worse than Zeus had suspected. For the first time, he started to think he'd been better off disdained.

"Now..." she continued. "You have the remaining character I requested?" she said. "On your person, I assume?"

The abrupt switch surprised him.

"The one from my former mistress?" The only one Hastings hadn't scrutinized, saying everything else looked to be in order and a man's bedroom proclivities should remain private. It was about the only thing the two of them had agreed upon. "Aye. I have it."

But Zeus made no move to retrieve the missive from his pocket. Let the secretive chit ask for it. Better yet, let her come and fish it out.

"Bare your chest for me, please."

"What the—" While Zeus' tongue floundered, his lower body speculated whether she'd desire buckskins be eliminated next. Wayward loins!

Not that he minded disrobing, not when the urge struck him. Which it hadn't. Not here, in this dismally cheerful room with its sweetly shabby furnishings and appallingly intriguing owner.

On second thought... "Why, if you please? If I'm to disrobe in front of someone *I've* yet to see, much less been formally introduced to, I'd like to be given a compelling reason."

And he hoped she supplied a damn good one because his fingers were now itching to reach for the buttons on his waistcoat.

"I would... I would see the chest of the man I think to take as husband."

Up to this point, only one person had been in control of everything—Lady Scandal. By way of Hastings, she had his name, his references, his financial worth...everything but the bloody measurement of his drawers. To be frank, she had his ballocks in her grasp, and what did he have in return? Only her deuced advertisement and the anticipation of Amherst. And an insatiable curiosity about the woman, one just begging to be appeased.

So, she wanted to see his nude torso? "As far as reasons go, it's not the strongest," he mused, fingers tapping along buttons, "but I could be amenable to an exchange of forfeits."

"An exchange?"

Zeus contemplated. There were four items of clothing to be discarded before his chest was bare. What might she be willing to relinquish for each of them? "I'll remove my tailcoat in exchange for one of your slippers."

After an expectant moment, one dainty slipper sailed over the partition and landed at his feet. His fingers flew in their haste and his tailcoat met the back of the settee.

"Your other slipper for my waistcoat."

"Ahh... I have but the one." She replied in a whisper that only raised more questions than it answered.

"One slipper? Or..." Something he'd not considered... "One *foot*?"

3

APPLICANT TWENTY-FOUR BARES ALL (OR NEARLY SO)

"Two feet!" Several giggled snorts, then a full-out gust of jocularity burst free, the sounds twisting something in his gut. "I assure you!"

Curious. "Then…your stocking in exchange for my waistcoat."

Silence.

Too bold?

Nay. For there came the light rustle of skirts being lifted, of silk descending…the envisioned sight of a creamy thigh…

Then *victory*, as one pale pink stocking soared gallantly toward him. His right arm shot out to halt its journey, rough fingers snagging on the delicate treasure.

Zeus wound his arm in a flying arc, twining the silk stocking over the back of his hand and leaving his fingers free to make short work of his waistcoat.

Once off, he flung it beside his discarded tailcoat. Eyes narrowed, he stared at the damnable screen, wishing he could see the vexing prize beyond. Debating just what he'd ask for next.

For though he could easily put an end to their little game, dispense with her vexing show of mystery, Zeus found he more than liked the idea of a potential wife being willing to indulge in a bit of risqué bawdiness. It bode well for their union.

If you can convince her to wed a bastard.

His fist tightened on the sultry stocking, trying to strangle out the nagging voice of reason. *If she'll have you, once she knows all.*

There was the rub, he realized, as the words of the great, doomed Hamlet rang like a gong against his conscience. *To sleep: perchance to dream: ay, there's the rub.*

Did he dare dream she'd have him?

JULIET NEVER DREAMED a man such as the one before her would respond to her advertisement. Just a fraction shy of haughty, a shade away from arrogant, his confident stature and striking countenance attracted her mightily. She stroked her newly bared toes across the wood floor, her gaze transfixed on the man in shirtsleeves breathing hard in the center of her sitting room.

When he'd first strutted into her sanctum, in no way could she have anticipated how her interview with applicant twenty-four would go. As it was, she feared she might be half in love already, given his oft-impertinent yet altogether candid replies. He certainly wasn't one to quibble or evade. Nor did he balk at conversing with females. That alone nigh earned him a spot in her heart.

And now...*now* viewing his bare chest was but a garment or two away, she realized as a streak of awareness settled between her thighs, causing her to again squiggle in place.

She awaited his next proposed forfeit exchange, the thrilling thrumming he created in her growing. "Mr. Tanner?" she prodded. "What shall we trade next?"

"Have you another stocking on?"

"Nay."

The strong column of his neck worked when he swallowed. "Petticoats? A shift? Stays?"

"Aye." *Though how will I get the last off by myself?* "Which would you like to claim in exchange for your neckcloth?" Then, to preserve modesty she wasn't feeling but knew she ought, Juliet added, "Although just because you request it may not make it so. There must remain some level of uncertainty even between courting couples, wouldn't you suppose?"

He threw back his head and laughed. And laughed. When he was done, his gaze again speared her through the screen. "Is that what we're doing? *Courting?*"

"In a manner of speaking."

"Very well. Courting." Though his lips still quirked with humor, his voice was as solid as a mountain. "To answer your question, I would not choose to have any measure of uncertainty between myself and my spouse. Uncertainty nor screens nor unnecessary clothing." He brought one hand to the simple knot at his neck. "What do I want for this? Ahh…let me think."

She watched Mr. Tanner contemplate their next exchange as though the weight of the world rested upon what he posed. He paced a tight circle around the table. Then another, his gaze sweeping from her hiding place to the doorway Jacks and Wivy had left through, a smattering of *hmmms* escaping his throat.

Instead of completing a third revolution as she thought he might, he swung around and his Hessians clipped confidently across the room. *Toward the exit.* She choked back a cry. He couldn't leave! Not now!

"Mr. Tanner!" Juliet protested, her spine going rigid, her entire body listing forward as though she could reach him through the screen and stop his retreat. “Don’t go! Please!”

“Go?” he said casually over one shoulder, still moving inexorably away. “Who said anything about going?” He paused at the closed door and made a great show of slowly turning the lock.

The resulting snick was quiet enough that Jacks failed to hear.

Vastly relieved Mr. Tanner had, instead of exiting the premises as she’d feared, locked himself *in*, she sank back into her chair.

“What do I want for my neckcloth?” he repeated again, one hand worrying the silk knot above his collar. A mischievous grin on his formidable face, he prowled forward, stopping once he reached his previous spot on the rug. He stared directly through the waterfall before giving the neckcloth a final flick. “Nothing. Not a blasted thing. However, I am willing to grant you my *shirt* for your *dress*.”

She stifled the automatic squeak of dismay. Neckcloth aside, once his shirt was gone, she’d see him, know if he possessed the form she’d dreamed of and longed for. *And you'll also be a garment or two away from being a total wicked wanton!* Mayhap, but was not *Scandal*ous her new name? With an increasing sense of naughtiness guiding her tongue and actions, Juliet replied, "Just so. But you shall go first this time and toss your garment to me."

Before she finished, he was struggling to push his neckcloth out of the way so he could lift the shirt over his head. Too agitated to watch the battle—in truth, too overcome by the sight of the decisive ridge growing more distinct at the front of his breeches—she squeezed her eyes shut. *I will not act missish. I will not swoon from excitement. I will not—*

Her efforts were hampered—nay, destroyed—when warm linen landed directly upon her head.

"Your turn, I believe," his rough voice intoned as the crisp, woodsy scent of bergamot suffused her senses, seduced away her remaining sense. "My lady? I await your dress."

Juliet eased his shirt away from her face. "And so you shall have it."

She wore a simple day dress, one fastened with buttons below her nape and made fitted by the sash beneath her breasts. Loosening her grip on his shirt and keeping her eyes downcast—for fear he wouldn't live up to her imaginings?—she leaned forward to undo both buttons and bow with fingers that fumbled.

"Have you cried coward?" he asked silkily, and it sounded as though he'd moved toward her. "Changed your mind?"

"Nay!" she choked out, ordering her fingers to firm up and cooperate. Though she lacked a dedicated one at present, Juliet informed him, "There's a reason ladies have maids, Mr. Tanner! Our attire isn't meant—"

"Shall I come round and assist?"

"Nay! Stay where you are!" Finally the long end of the sash whispered free. "Please do not move, not yet."

"Panic not, dear one. For now, I shall impatiently await your offering."

"Aye, please." Remaining seated, she shuffled her weight from hip to hip and awkwardly tugged until the dress slid beyond her posterior. Then she whipped it up and over her head as fast as humanly possible, mussing the prim knot she'd tamed this morning beyond redemption.

Emerging from the dark cocoon of her dress, Juliet was reminded of a chrysalis bursting forth into a splendorous butterfly—one with a slightly broken wing—and resolved to put aside any remaining reticence, to do away with her nettlesome nerves. If, as she was beginning to surmise, she'd found the man she intended to call husband, then did she not owe it to herself to enjoy the remainder of their "interview" to its absolute fullest?

Straightening her spine and swinging her head back like a sauce-box, she found his face through the screen. "There. It is off."

He advanced two steps, then stopped, his nostrils flaring.

Could he, too, smell her desire?

Her eyes longed to drop below his chin; maidenly uncertainty held them in place.

Despite her focus on that granite feature, with its chiseled indentation surrounded by a faint shadow of whiskers, she made out the massacre of his neckcloth, one long end swaying across an expanse of chest so broad—

She looked.

Looked and gasped. For not five feet from her, nearly bare, save for the rumpled silk bisecting it, was the finest example of manly beauty Juliet could've conceived. The lightly furred, ridged muscles stretching across and tapering down were sun-darkened. Just inside his hip bones, dual shadowed indentions disappearing into his buckskins tempted her fingers to learn *his* hidden secrets. The arms tensed at his sides were no different, sculpted shoulders and biceps beckoning her forward.

Oh, to have those arms wrapped around her, to be held against such a formidable display of strength and grandeur. To lay her troubles at his feet and have him slay dragons alongside her… Aye, this was the man she chose.

"And what"—her voice sounded hushed to her own ears—"shall I grant you in exchange for your neckcloth?"

. . .

"YOUR FACE," Zeus told her, resolved. To be this hard, aching this fiercely for a wench he'd yet to see? One who'd led—nay, *continued to lead*—him on a dreadfully merry chase? "It's the outside of enough, madam! I would see you now. Your face, your hair, your breas—" The word he hadn't meant to utter aloud strangled off when she emerged from behind the screen.

More petite than he'd expected, given her force of personality, he struggled to take in everything about her at once. Critically so, for at first glance, Zeus feared he was doomed.

Doomed to crave her the rest of his days.

Her nose was too long, her chin too pointed. Lips too narrow. And eyes? Definitely too expressive. The blue-grey of a churning sky before a tempest, they matched the thunderous, late-day clouds pressing in beyond the raised windowpane. Blinking up at him with uncertainty and appreciation and desire...

Aye, definitely desire.

"Lady Juliet Ashland," she said by way of introduction, curtsying with care. Twin spots of color blazed from her cheeks and she angled her head to hold his gaze while lowering her body. "I am honored to meet you, Mr. Tanner. Very honored."

Despite features his analytical mind thought anything but perfect, she appeared perfectly adorable to him, her allure only enhanced by how she openly admired him, as though he, too, exceeded her expectations.

As his pride—among other things—inflated under her regard, two additional items registered at once.

First, that the glorious sunset hair, trapped in a disastrously uneven knot hanging near one shoulder, was the finest he'd ever seen, calling forth his fingers to ensnare themselves in it from here 'til infinity, and secondly— "Your leg! It's splinted!"

In little more than shift and stays, she straightened and hobbled toward him, bracing part of her weight on a simple axillary crutch. "Glad I am to note your powers of observation."

He strode forward and scooped her against his chest, the crutch crashing to the floor.

No sooner did it land than Jacks hollered through the door. "Milady? Has the bounder overstepped?"

"Have I?" Zeus inquired in a whisper, hefting her in his arms.

The color on her cheeks blazed hotter. "Nay."

She threw her arms around his neck as he carried her to the settee, leaving Zeus confounded as to why she'd hide her person—when she possessed such a devilishly pleasing exterior—and speculating how soon he could taste the narrow, tremulous smile that tempted more than any lush pout.

"Milady?!" The manservant banged on the door.

"'Tis nothing!" she called out as Zeus carefully placed her upon the cushion. He fancied she stroked one hand down his bare chest before he stood upright. "Now leave off your duties for the night, Jacks! 'Tis an order!"

Zeus stepped back, rounding the low table. He had to because if he tasted her now, he wouldn't stop until he'd licked all of her and his eyes weren't done yet. Not even close.

"Lady Juliet, the honor is all mine." He bowed, ridiculous with his neckcloth dangling before him, but necessary nevertheless, for here—despite the tangled hair and improper (no thanks to him) attire, despite the appalling habit of asking after his faults, despite the brazenness to trade clothes with a stranger—was the "lady" he'd never truly thought to claim for his own.

The one he couldn't wait to make his.

"Z. J. Tanner, *yours*..." He returned to his full height, for once keeping his expression diffident. "Dare I hope for the rest of the evening, and possibly the rest of our lives?"

As if that reminded her of what brought them together, she nodded decisively and arranged herself, shift, stays and all, as demurely as any maiden. Cheeks still pinker than he would've predicted, given what she'd required of him so far *and* willingly forfeited in exchange, she captured his gaze and bid, "Please read your remaining character reference."

"My what?" He couldn't have heard aright.

"The character. From your mistress."

"Read it? Out loud? *To you?*" When his erection now strained his buckskins, when his nostrils were so filled with her scent he couldn't breathe without taking her in?

"I fail to see anyone else in the room."

When he was half ready to do anything she asked, his debatable birthright be damned, just because he desired to bed her? Yearned to wed her? "Nay!"

Stormy eyes flashed to his. "Aye. I want to hear her words in your voice."

If he hadn't caught the faint quiver in hers, or so Zeus told himself, he wouldn't have done it.

Wouldn't have retrieved the letter from the pocket of his tailcoat, brushing against her nude shoulder intentionally as he leaned over to do so, before retreating a respectable distance—Respectable? Hah!—where he unfolded the parchment, saw again the words written with so much unfathomable glee it made him cringe to remember, and *willingly* overlooked the sting to his dignity. "Ahem-hem." Grit seared his throat, as if his body knew what it was about to audibly announce and sought to stop him. "Ahh-hemmm!"

Either that or maybe it was the blasted scone still making its presence known.

"Arrhhhh-hemm."

"Mr. Tanner? Shall you proceed or shall I request Wivy rejoin us?" As if she would! Juliet would no sooner put a halt to their intimate encounter than she would force Mr. Tanner to do anything so obviously abhorrent to him—*if* she had any other choice.

Which she didn't, not in this instance. She had to know what his lovers thought of his swiving prowess. "I'd rather not, but if I must, in order to secure your cooperation for the remainder of our interview..."

As though her empty threat loosened his tongue, he heartedly began reciting the words on the page. "*I, Marianna Longley, currently of*

Torrington House, Surrey, do declare Zeus Tanner—"

"Zeus?" Juliet laughed as she said it, the surprising syllable tickling her tongue. "That's your given name?"

It was either laugh or take to the floor in a faint. She'd never been so close to a man she found so harshly appealing.

His features were bold, definitely too severe to be considered handsome, classically or otherwise. But the fierce expression in his eyes drew her as nothing else. Screen, modesty and modest attire so far gone she couldn't conceive ever wanting them back.

"It is," he said so haughtily she could well believe he commanded a pantheon of gods. "Does it displease you? That the...*bastard* son of a *maid* would be granted something so illustrious, so far above his station?"

"Nay! I adore it, truly!" Sobering, she allowed her gaze to roam over defiant features that undoubtedly expected her to find fault with his humble origins, to eagerly skim over muscles worthy of Hercules and any earthly task. Then she stared intently into his eyes. A brilliant blue, she saw now. They shone like the eye of a peacock feather, reminding her of those majestic beauties that once strutted over the grounds of Amherst...but no longer. The bittersweet memory softened her voice. "Zeus. It suits you, for no name could be stronger. Fit for a king, it is."

His complexion turned ruddy. "Aye. That's what Mum always said—better to be king of the gods than king of a paltry country."

"And I daresay she was right. Ruling mere mortals on Earth cannot compare to the inhabitants of Olympus."

His shimmering eyes narrowed, as if to stop her from seeing into his soul. "And my birth?"

"What of it?"

ZEUS COULDN'T DECIDE if she mocked him with her casual disregard or if his disgraceful beginnings were truly of no consequence. "The notion of wedding a bastard doesn't degrade you? Make your tongue trip over itself in your haste to order me evicted?"

"Nothing could be further from my thoughts, I assure you." A lift of russet brows accompanied her earnest reply. "I've learned the measure of a man is in how he treats others, not what title he may or may not possess, and certainly not things in which he had no say or control over. Your letter? Please continue."

Stupefied by her calm acceptance of what he'd dreaded as his final obstacle, never anticipating a lady of rank would acknowledge him without exhaustive convincing, Zeus made an effort to find his tongue, pry it off the floor where it'd dropped along with his jaw, and employ it with the same aplomb she exhibited. "*...declare Zeus Tanner to be a most generous and thoughtful lover. His praiseworthy actions before the...act...*" He stumbled here, recalling the gaiety with which Marianna had written this part. "*...are dampening in the extreme. He will set his sights—*"

"Pardon me," Lady Juliet interrupted, a quizzical expression replacing the encouraging one of before. "She deems it a tribute to call your efforts 'dampening'?"

He stared. Was she in jest? "What?"

She leaned away from the settee, the skin between her eyebrows creasing. "Her...ardor..." Now *she* stumbled. Then forged ruthlessly ahead. "You dampen it? And yet she praises you?"

Good God. He'd known the lecher she was married to. It was inconceivable. But... "Are you an innocent?"

Rather than answer, she bit one corner of her mouth and relaxed back into the cushions, crossing, then uncrossing her arms and looking everywhere but at him. "Well?" Zeus demanded into the strained silence. "Are you in truth a virgin?"

Not that it made any difference to him; he wanted her, was beginning to think she *needed* him.

Hell. It did make a difference. A big one.

A *lady* for a wife. A virgin bride.

Fate had surely smiled on him for once. But how to convince her *he* was the husband she required without having to reveal the rest of this damnable letter?

. . .

Her own spirits dampened now that she'd inadvertently betrayed her ignorance, Juliet sought to cover the blunder by feigning confidence. "I was married to one of the crudest men in England for all of three years. What do you think?"

She finally brought her eyes back to his magnificent chest, her mouth going dry at the sight. Hair. Who knew a man could have such a glorious feathering of silky hair upon his sculpted musculature? Traveling across the textured plains of his stomach, past his navel and down...down...

"I think your husband was the worst of men. A hard-arsed, bracket-faced buffoon. A reprobate and a bastard in the worst possible sense." As though stunned by hearing the oaths spewing from his mouth, Mr. Zeus Tanner tensed his jaw, inclined his head in a brief bow. "Forgive me. *I think*, regardless of whatever experience you claim to have, you've never been bedded properly."

"And you know how to do that? Bed me...properly?"

His head came up, eyes flashing fire. "I most certainly do!"

"Please go on."

"With...bedding you?" he said raggedly.

Juliet gave a negative shake of her head. "With your reading."

She thought she heard him mutter "I'd rather get right to the bedding" before he plainly said, "In truth, I'll do most anything to postpone finishing this letter."

"Most anything?" Juliet sought confirmation. Dare she ask what kept crossing her mind? Oh, it was too brazen by half! Wivy would be aghast to learn Juliet risked her already shaky reputation (ruined by running the advertisement in the first place, according to Wivy) to request such a thing.

Who says Wivy must know? She's not here any longer, now is she?

But you are. And he is.

And oh, merciful heavens, he was so very big and brawny, his powerful muscles so spectacular. His sun-lightened hair and sun-darkened body the complete opposite of Leth's scrawny, whey-toned self and slouchy stature.

"Aye," he said assuredly, likely having no clue what manner of wicked thoughts now danced temptingly through her head. "You've already tested my mettle with your higgledy-piggledy array of questions, my taste buds with your huckster of a scone and my patience with your confounding ability to prevaricate. Why not test me further?" He ended on a relaxed laugh. "What would you have me do? Or answer? Though my current ensemble is certainly not fit for king nor court, I remain most *court*eously at your service."

His glib-tongued wordplay tempted a smile, but the compulsion to see more of him stript to skin prevented her from responding in kind. "Would you..."

"Would I what?"

"Would you...mayhap...consent to... Oh blazes! Forget I asked. Or didn't ask." She huffed a sigh. "I pray you will forgive the interruption. Now do go on with her letter."

. . .

"No. I want to know what you want of me." *Anything* to avoid completing the dreadful letter. Only the sheerest of will allowed Zeus to refrain from crushing it in his fist. "Would I… what? Come now, if we're seriously contemplating a union between us, should there not be freedom to speak? Regardless of topic?"

"Aye, I would wish for that as well. Though I confess it is not a freedom that's been granted me in the past."

"I am granting it now. Inquire away."

Again she hesitated, her eyes skittering like a scared rabbit, jumping all over the place but returning time and again to the area below his waist. The area that, despite his best efforts, kept responding to her undisguised interest. "Lady Juliet?"

In a hushed voice, she quickly sped through, "Would you perchance show me your male part?"

The silence after her whispered request weighed on him like a quarry full of stone, slowing his thoughts, stalling his response.

Zeus was hard-pressed not to snap his fingers in front of his ears, to test their acuity. To bang a flat palm upside his head. Had he heard her aright?

As if to tell him he had, the far-off grumble of thunder reached his awareness easily enough. It sounded like encouraging applause. And why should that surprise him? The Baseborn Bastard and Lady Scandal were putting on a grand show.

"Did you not hear me?" She blinked up at him with equal parts sincerity, curiosity and, it looked to him, pure mortification. "Could you be persuaded to lower your buckskins and show me your...your..."

"My male part," he choked out, finishing what she couldn't bring herself to utter a second time. "Aye, I heard you. I'm just attempting to ensure I understood. You...want..." He spoke clearly and plainly—possibly to shock the little she-devil clear to her toes? "To view my dirk? My cock? Now? Here? Have I got the right of it?"

"You do indeed."

As that unruly appendage responded to her honest, if outrageous, request and his mantra changed from brains over ballocks to ballocks *for* brains, Zeus actually debated showing it to her. "*Are you insane?* Bound for Bedlam on the next cart out?" he asked, his dismay not fabricated in the least, trying to convince them both just how asinine this was. "Am I? For still standing here—like this?"

Arms spread wide, with the blighted letter clenched in one outstretched hand, her pale stocking dangling from the other, and his silk neckcloth waving in front of his nude chest like a white flag of surrender, Zeus wanted to deliver a sharp slap to his deuced responsive *male part*, chastise it into calming down. Better yet, deliver several sharp slaps to *her* posterior to punish her for being so positively enchanting and without guile or guilt. To ask such a thing! And of a stranger!

Instead of administering that well-deserved smack to either his person or hers, Zeus waited…wondered…willed himself to ponder… what might Lady Scandal do next? "At least you're living up to your name, I'll give you that."

Her lips pursed and she sniffed as though something soiling the very air she breathed wafted in front of her nose. “There’s no call to be disparaging. I—”

“I meant it as a compliment.”

“You did?”

4

MAGNIFICENT PROTRUSIONS & MANLY PARAPHERNALIA

A COMPLIMENT?

Hell if he knew anymore. About any of this. "Aye, I did. I like your gumption, woman—and before you reprimand me for any perceived slight, I know full well the honor you do me, reflecting upon my suit. It escapes me not that your inherent place in society elevates you so far above my reach you might as well reside in the heavens. As a man of no birth, no military accomplishments and nothing to recommend him save several heartfelt references and my own desire to claim your hand, I owe you deference and humility and should accord you every respect that is mind to command. Yet I tell you now—when we're alone, if you act the part of a refined lady, so shall I treat you as one. If, on the other hand, you behave—"

"If I do not?" she interrupted his tirade. "What then?" Her cheeks flushed again but this time 'twas not embarrassment nor timidity. No…'twas the flush of excitement, perhaps one of anger, that heated her skin and brought a spark to her eyes. "Perhaps I want to be treated as a female, *as a woman*, when we're alone. No more, no less. What say you, Mr. Zeus Tanner?"

How could he say anything when some inner sense told him this was the first time she'd allowed her mouth to unburden her tongue?

"Would you treat a *wife* as one or the other but not both? Mayhap a *lady*"—the word dripped distain like venom from a viper—"thinks of her birth as blighted as you do your own, have you paused once to consider that? Mayhap a lady is trapped beneath both convention and propriety, strapped down by responsibilities and duty to those relying on her to the very detriment of her own self, her *womanly* self!"

Eyes flashing fire, she pierced him with her sincerity, her wish to be anything other than what she'd been born—a L-A-D-Y.

Both hands flexed with the need to touch the womanly lady before him, but he restrained the urge. Crinkling the letter in one and tightening his grip upon the stocking with the other, he remained resolutely silent, resolutely in place, instinctively granting her the freedom she'd been denied previously, that of airing her grievances against the very sex that sought to dominate and control her.

"Have you ever, even for one second, given any thought to the plight of a young, aristocratic female, one locked by the unfortunate circumstance of her 'exalted' birth into a marriage—a union—not of her choosing? Well, by all that's good and holy, I will *choose* this time!"

Though bridled (she'd not raised her voice sufficiently to reach beyond the confines of the room), her very intensity screamed at him, each syllable slamming into his ears, pounding through his blood, and settling into his loins, weighing his staff with desire, and him with the desire to answer her in kind—as a *man*, and not as her social inferior. Two human beings, one male, one female, choosing to forsake the boundaries and strictures of the world to which they both belonged in order to reach an accord, together.

In any other scenario, save this mad one she'd constructed amid solicitors and servants and shields, two strangers would never have such an occasion to talk and behave as freely, as scandalously, as they each continued to do so.

That he stood before her, both attracted and appalled, more riveted than repulsed, spoke volumes as to how badly he wanted *her*. Lady Juliet. Her fire, her boldness, her pointy little chin and plump little breasts. As her heat and vivacity continued to warm him, thoughts of revenge faded to the background; images of her, challenging his head and warming his bed, surged to the foreground.

"I will choose!" she repeated hotly. "Because—Because…" Her breath caught as a single, stifled sob worked free. Brandishing her arms in front of her as though warding off bad memories, she breathed deeply.

When her splinted leg shifted, tipping her forward, Zeus feared her balance was soon to follow. He jumped toward her to assist.

Shaking her head, she motioned him back.

After several inhalations, she regained the control she'd lost for so short a time. Pressing her spine into the settee, she speared him with her earnest gaze. "I will choose my next spouse because I refuse to live with doubt and fear and regret for the rest of my life. If this marriage scheme fails to procure me the right husband, it won't be for lack of trying. Or for lack of trying something different! Now... I acknowledge that my request is beyond the pale, beyond the bounds of everything and anything considered acceptable on any level of society, but...but the dreaded...*ridge* above your...your...*below* your waist has captured my attention thoroughly and I crave the sight of you, yearn to see what manner of man you might be."

As though acceding to her impassioned plea, the wrinkled letter drifted from his grasp.

To prevent its escape, Zeus tightened his stranglehold on the stocking. Too bad his mind had already flown the coop, his sane thoughts scattering like wayward chickens.

More like a cocky rooster, his damn cock only wanted to do her bidding.

She gazed up at him, enraptured, granting him a look of such pure adoration, Zeus had the ghastly feeling he could spend the rest of his life living up to the image of the man he *could* be in her sight but would never attain if he retained pride and walked away now.

"For God's sake, stop looking at me like that!" *Brains over ballocks*, he chanted. *Mind over mattress.*

"I cannot help it," she admitted with breathless abandon, motioning toward his randy rooster. "You appear so very...*decisive* where Letheridge was...was nothing but a wan imitation." She lowered her voice as though confiding the veriest of secrets. "He really possessed a wimpy winkle, if you must know."

A growl scraped up his throat. He didn't. He didn't need to know.

"Please?" So earnest, so innocently excited in her entreaty. As he stood there, wavering, her eyes grew big and round. "I have it! I'll trade you my petticoats for a glimpse of your masculine protrusion," she finished on an embarrassed, brazen whisper.

But Zeus could no longer appreciate her adorably inviting and horribly inappropriate offer. He was too busy appreciating the delicate length of leg visible beneath her shift as she hastily untied and shucked the layers of petticoats bound round her waist.

Allowing the last one to fall free on either side of her now discernible hips, she beamed up at him, bright-eyed and rosy-cheeked. "There! I've done it. 'Tis your turn now. Show me your manly projection. Your—"

Afraid of what she might call it next, Zeus interrupted. "Good God, will you stop? My male part. My manly projection. My masculine *protrusion*? So you want to see my cock? If you want to see it, you damn well better be able to say—"

"Aye!" She stared at him defiantly, determinedly, as if his crude language didn't put her off in the least. "Your cock. Your pr-prick! Your phallus. Your sword, bayonet, yard, bodkin, dagger, dirk. Your *penis*," she enunciated clearly, her fingers knotting over themselves in her bid to appear unaffected, "and if you want me to say more, then I'm afraid I shall disappoint because I'm completely out of euphemisms or naming knowledge in that particular arena. But I do so still desire to *see* it."

"Fine!" His hands went to the fall of his buckskins. "Fine! Good Lord, woman—" Fast, furious, his fingers undid the buttons on either side. "Fine, I say! Do not ever let it be thought I am not an accommodating applicant! By God, you'd try the patience of a saint." Bracing his legs, he reached past his drawers to grasp his turgid rod. Keeping hand and dirk concealed, giving himself a sharp squeeze—and his brain one more chance to reconsider—he hesitated. He stood there and he stalled, nostrils flared, mind striving for the right course, lungs heaving as if he were a stallion scenting a mare. His mare. And perhaps he was.

"A saint," he pondered aloud, contemplating, Do I leave now, abandon all hope of gaining Amherst and the lovely lady who possesses it but walk away with a modicum of pride intact?

Or do I remain and bare all…in every sense imaginable? The truth, my body, my longing… The urges storming his staff anything but saintly, Zeus concluded, "And yet, I have never been accused of being one of their exalted number."

She watched him, eyes flared, the hard point of her nipples thrusting upward with each of her ragged inhalations, the tiny beads visible through the thin lawn, that deuced corset cinched round her middle only enhancing the gentle swells.

Every speck of her attention centered on his wrist where his hand had disappeared beneath his waistband. His straining erection grew impossibly thicker, stiffened to the point of pain when the tip of her tongue darted out as she licked her lips, giving him but a glimpse of one part of her he intended to explore thoroughly—the tempting cavern of her mouth.

Her squeak of excitement was nearly his undoing. At the sound, his damn shaft jumped within the confining circle of his fingers and nearly poked a hole in his buckskins. But it was her hoarse cry of, “Please. Please do not make me wait any longer. I so crave the sight of you,” that convinced him to stop debating the merits of morality versus the sins of sexuality and release the death grip on his dagger after one final near strangulation at the root. Using both hands, he shoved down his drawers and buckskins.

“There!”

Throwing back his shoulders and anchoring fists at his waist, he balanced in place, proudly, awkwardly, awaiting her reaction.

Her prim nod of approval, her scream of outrage or possibly a graceful swoon—none of those would have surprised him at this point. Of course she wouldn’t respond as one might predict, not his Lady Scandal.

As he weaved on unsteady feet, his engorged dirk jutting toward her position on the settee like a dowsing rod divining heaven, what did she do but sweep both palms to her flushed cheeks, open her eyes as wide as they’d go, and breathlessly exclaim, “Oh my. Oh-oh-my. It’s—You’re—much more *solid* than I expected.”

Hands hiding the bulk of her awed expression, she cocked her head as if that slight tilt would enable her to view him better. His damn hips preened under the unexpected admiration, twisting to the side so she could view him in partial profile.

“Longer too,” she murmured appraisingly, regaining her voice in light of his willingness—stupidness?—to allow her to look her fill. “Undeniably longer when not constrained. Mercy. Definitely bigger. Gracious me.” She finally tore her eyes from his bobbing bauble and blinked up at him. “I must admit, your virile attribute is decidedly more…intriguing than I… Just… *Oh!*” And there she went, flailing her hands in front of her face as though to prevent that swoon he’d been expecting all along.

Virile attribute? At least she’d progressed from the mouthful of Ms and Ps she’d massacred and pelted his anatomy with moments before.

Buckskins bunched just above his knees, a draft threatening to wilt his erection, he braved her scrutiny. Draft? Nay, more likely *daft*, the foolishness of this entire encounter superseding any errant air currents whistling through the drafty abode.

He was daft to be standing here when she was so far away, that was a certainty. Ready to remedy that and quickly, Zeus took one bungling step toward her.

“Nay! Not yet.” She scooted back, trying to merge into the settee, exhibiting another unmistakable hint of shyness. One of very few, his beleaguered brain had to concede.

She pointed to the floor where he stood. “Please stay there, where you are.” Her fingertips flew to cover her mouth, then she brought them down and tangled them together. “I desire to look from…from afar.”

“Bloody amazing.” How she could sit there, cheeks blazing, eyes glued to his dirk, hands now working frantically at the loose fabric of her shift as though they wanted to be on *him* and, conversely, she was doing everything humanly possible to occupy them elsewhere? Anxiety, boldness and bashfulness, all wrapped up in the most delightful package to ever cross his path.

Damn daftness aside, how could he be so bloody hot, boiling on the inside, standing there nearly naked in her drafty abode? It had to be her enticing company, for it certainly wasn't their surroundings. So she wanted to look from afar? Didn't yet want to touch? Maybe he could hurry her along...

"Why don't you stroke me—with your mouth?"

"Stroke you with...my...mouth?" she repeated in a whisper as if she was working through what he meant. He knew the second realization dawned. "Really? Touch it—with my lips? My tongue?"

Though her forehead creased in dismay at the idea, Zeus caught the swift licking of her lower lip, that pink tongue slipping out to slick over it before venturing toward the tiny vee centered on the top. Her lips glistened after its journey; his dagger grew heavier still. Her mind might be rebelling at the thought of trying something so very wanton, so womanly, but the rest of her was obviously intrigued, her ladylike sensibilities unable to stifle the carnal awareness arcing between them.

"Aye. One of the many varied sexual pleasures we can share in the marriage bed or out of it—I'm not particular *where* I taste your charms—has to do with licking each other."

"Licking each other..." Uttered as though the idea was completely foreign. "Where exactly? Just...there?"

"Certainly here." His fingers found their way back to his staff. He supported its weight, palm up, as though humbly giving her an offering.

The heat of his shaft seared through the silk stocking wrapped about his hand. Zeus steeled himself not to groan at the sight. His hardened, elongated flesh displayed upon pale pink, served up for her approval—or disapproval—like a trophy presented before a queen.

Watching him with rapt attention, she gave an involuntary whimper when he circled his fingers and pumped himself.

"You could lick me all along here," Zeus pointed out, easing his tightened fist along his erection with excruciating slowness, the whispered hiss of silk against his skin echoed by his mouth.

Like a lightning strike, the unexpected decadence of her sultry stocking caressing his flesh ripped through him. Flashed white-hot through his being and ballocks. When he reached the tip, he grazed his thumb across the slit, barely avoiding a whimper of his own. "Here too. But there are other places I might enjoy being licked or might enjoy licking you."

"Such as?"

"The side of your neck."

As though feeling his tongue upon her person, she brought one restless hand up to her neck and caressed several fingers down the side. "Mmmm."

"Behind your ear. The inside of your dainty wrist. Your breasts...your nipples."

With each place he mentioned, her own fingers trailed behind, caressing the spots in lieu of his tongue, but just before alighting upon one of her breasts, they fluttered in the air. Again she brought them to her sides and bundled them in her shift. Her gaze skittered away from his. "All right, but not yet. I'm not ready to lick you. Not right now."

"Very well. I can be patient. Enjoy the anticipation." If it didn't do him in.

That brought her eyes back to his, one sunset brow arched in surprise. "You can? I thought *impatience* was one of your strengths, not the other way around."

"When it comes to tasting and savoring your body? Or offering mine up for your dining pleasure? Consider me Job, my lady."

A shy smile toyed with her lips before she chastised, "For shame, Mr. Tanner, bringing a scion of the Good Book into this wicked interlude."

"'Tis not wicked if we wed. And did I not already tell you—I'm no saint." To emphasize his claim, his fist pumped faster along his pained shaft, drawing her attention back to what she'd asked to see.

She stared intently at his actions a moment, then bounced her focus up to his chest. "Nay, one would never be charged with accusing you of behaving saintly."

"Then we're agreed?"

She gave a light laugh, once again meeting his gaze. “On what? That you’re an impatient wretch?”

“That I may step forth and begin my licking exploration of you, but that yours of me may be postponed.” *Pray God, let us be agreed.*

The smile faltered, then fell. “We certainly are not agreed upon that, nothing of the sort!”

“Pity. I’d hoped we’d reached such an accord, but alas”—he gave a hearty sigh—“as we have not, I refuse to stand here, such as I am, any longer.”

The moment he released his beleaguered bauble and reached for his buckskins, she exclaimed, “No, wait!”

“Aye?” Without making any effort to rise or continue the motion of modesty, he held his position, knowing the extended length of his deuced “male part” continued to fascinate her, the constant glimpses she attempted to sneak at his primed penis despite her own modest restraint obvious indeed. “If exchanging intimate kisses is not on your immediate agenda, then there exists no need for me to remain in such a state of...*déshabillé.*"

Intentionally, he tossed the feminine word at her. Let her think standing there made him uncomfortable. Let guilt begin to creep over her at the way she treated him. No need to grant her the knowledge of how very much posing brazenly before her—his prim little lady—nearly nude and at her mercy, had excited and aroused. Had banished his initial discomfort to the dungeons. Definitely no need for her to see how close to eruption her uninhibited appreciation of his anatomy made him.

"THERE DOES!" Juliet exclaimed, seeking the words to convince him. "There exists every need to remain as you are."

She couldn't bear for him to mask the masculine attributes she was only now growing bold enough to stare at without flushing. "There exists every reason, I assure you!"

"Is that the way of it, eh?" The beautiful scoundrel remained hunched, poised to return his clothing to their rightful, respectful place. Close to laughing at her if she wasn't mistaken. "Then why, pray, am I not hearing a litany of convincing ones? Your mouth remains mighty mute on the subject at hand, my lady."

Mayhap so, but Juliet definitely noticed the change in timbre, the slight wavering of his voice, as he'd just murmured *at hand*. She'd caught the subtle tightening of his now empty fists and the way the thick column of his majestic male part gave a tiny jump toward her, as though defying his efforts to tuck it away.

Aye, he might bait and banter, might hint at wanting to end his current salacious situation, but Juliet suspected he found their illicit exchange as invigorating as she did. Nevertheless, because she knew by now he was a man who appreciated a good and hearty debate, she granted him her rationale. Anything to prolong the splendidly wicked view. "Reason one, I have yet to look my fill. Stand up straight again, if you would," she commanded as imperiously as she'd been taught, "so I may see it—you—more clearly. Aye, like that. Reason two, the concept of...of... intimate lickage might be one with which I was previously unaware so my reticence is understandable, nay expected. I am a lady, you know." Oh, but surely she was not acting as one.

Juliet was swiftly discovering the joys to be had in forsaking the restrictive upbringing she'd been smothered with since birth. Bah, other than talent with a needle and foreign languages, what had her unsolicited birthright into high society ever gained her? Only an even more restrictive spouse and lonely existence, accompanied by a mountain of debt when said spouse choked and croaked.

That and several unwanted, up-close visuals of Leth's pasty groin and floppy appendage before he'd moved on and taken up residence in his new underground abode.

Really, the tedious toad had even forced her to touch it a time or twelve. *Blech.*

Fulfilling her duty as a dutiful wife, she might have done so at the time without heated protest. But Juliet now came to recognize the revulsion she'd suffered and suppressed, lacking, in her youth and naïveté, the courage or comfort to make her own wishes known.

What was the opposite of revulsion, she pondered, weighing her options—and the sight before her. Untethered delight? Sheer joy? A strong passion to discover more secrets of the male flesh?

She currently experienced those and more, evaluating Mr. Tanner and his attractively appealing attribute. The one she couldn't seem to avert her gaze from.

So he wanted reasons, did he?

Easy enough to supply, for she tasted a wealth of them upon her tongue. "Reason three, the only other manful prominence I've had the misfortune to be intimately acquainted with made my flesh crawl as though a thousand maggots creeped along every speck of my skin." Without intent, she scraped her palms down the tops of her thighs, wiping off the offensive memory for the last time. "Reason four, I find my curiosity about *yours* greater than I ever dared conceive and—"

"Thank God for that," he interrupted, standing tall and imposing, his fierce brows slashed over those shimmering sapphire eyes—in frustrated relief or disapproval, she couldn't tell which.

"Five. Just because I said no immediate...uh..."

"Licking? Suckling? *Tasting?*" he supplied, rather unhelpfully she thought as his words sent her mind and senses scattering in all sorts of naughty directions.

"Just so. Um... Does not mean I am not amenable to the possibility at some point in the near future."

"How near?"

How was it his length continued to expand? To thicken? To make her mouth water in ways even the veriest of roasted goose and Belgian chocolate failed to?

He was built so exquisitely. She yearned to explore every strong and powerful inch, from the tops of his broad, expansive shoulders, past the corded plane of his stomach, all the way down, down to those big, brawny thighs covered in just the lightest sheen of hair. *Exquisite* didn't do him justice, really...

As if watching someone else, Juliet saw her—for once—eager-to-touch hand lifting out, toward him. She recalled it, balling both together in her lap. Blazes! Her cheeks were on fire again. One would think another stormy, dreary afternoon would put to rest the heated response, but she swore her insides were sweltering, melting...

"Six!" she exclaimed, sensing another interruption looming, judging by the way a muscle in his jaw had started ticking. "I am at six, aren't I?" Without giving him a chance to complain, she rushed on. "Or if not, six and a half. Since reaching my majority, I have spent a good deal of time fearing the unknown. Observing you helps put that fear to ground."

"The unknown?"

Rather than respond to his guarded tone and corroborate his suspicions, Juliet realized other questions of the newly aroused mind must be answered. "Would you...ah..." *Oh just say it, Juliet! It's one thing for him to suspect you're an inexperienced ninny—it's another to confirm it outright!* "Please turn around."

"Like so?" Accompanied by the tiniest of grunts, Mr. Tanner complied, shuffling around in a tight circle, its journey completed so fast, she collected naught. No new information. No complete views.

"No! Not like that. Turn and pause, if you would. Facing away." Hearing it, her ears burned at what she requested. Juliet wanted to check the air beside her for smoke but feared if she took her eyes off Mr. Tanner, like a genie bound to dispense wishes, he might disappear once released. Or was that leprechauns? "Oh, would you just *please* grant me a view of your..."

What did she term it? His posterior? Backside? *Derrière*? What did one call their sit-upon in polite company? "Your hindquarters! I desire to see them, please."

His banked gaze narrowed. "You care for a glimpse of my arse?"

"Not so much a glimpse as a look. A, umm, *long* one."

She could see him calculating either a refusal or another demand of her clothing. Given how she possessed but the two remaining items—her tightly laced stays and gossamer shift beneath—Juliet cajoled, "For every moment you comply, I will give you another reason why it matters so very much."

"How could any man decry such an offer?"

As he started a breath-stealingly slow revolution, the muscles in his thighs straining and flexing, Juliet loosed the other, possibly most profound reason swirling about her mind. "Seven, I never, in all my wildest, most secret hopes and imaginings, thought to gaze upon such a magnificent sight of grandeur and grand proport—"

"Me?" He turned his head to the side to inquire, fairly preening like that peacock she'd thought of earlier. "Magnificent?"

"Yes, most assuredly you. And I beg you, beseech you, do not take the sight away from me. Not yet."

Silence settled between them, save for the increasing boom and blast of thunder as the storm exploded violently overhead. Paying no mind to its fury, Juliet inspected the *arse* of the man before her. Strong and gently curved, pale yet pleasing, the firm portion of his anatomy she'd never once thought to consider on any other beckoned her onward, as did his front. Tempted her to further wantonness—how might such inviting-looking flesh *feel*? To her hand, her lips?

But Rome wasn't built in a day, and multitudes of strictures weren't abandoned without effort, so when he spun back around to face her, in all his near-naked splendor, Juliet chose not to grumble.

After all, only a paper skull would complain about sampling the banquet Mr. Tanner allowed her to feast optically upon.

"Does it not prick your conscience, my lady, to reside there so composed and clothed while I stand here thus?"

Arms outstretched, silk neckcloth swaying, buckskins clumped over the tops of his tall boots, the wretch attempted to assume a pitiful, put-upon expression. Attempted and failed spectacularly. This man couldn't look pitiful if someone dipped him in a vat of pathetic and coated him with grimy goose feathers.

At the image—the one in her mind, of what she suspected Mr. Tanner *thought* he portrayed—Juliet laughed. Then laughed again. A less pitiful man she'd never seen! "Pardon me," she gasped out between grating giggles she couldn't seem to snaffle. "Your attempt to garner my sympathy is having the opposite effect, I fear."

Juliet bit down on both of her lips, compressing her smile as flat as she could, doing her best to harness the humor and exhibit a more dignified demeanor. For seriously, was this not a most serious occasion? Did not inspecting the, um, masculine paraphernalia of a potential husband warrant every bit as much the solemnity of one inspecting a horse?

Though she doubted any horse ever had hindquarters as fine as the ones she'd been given leave to evaluate.

And that thought set her off all over again.

For though she may not be overly familiar with horses, she did know stallions were prized for certain attributes. Attributes she had no doubt the man posturing before her in his altogether possessed in spades.

Grinning gamely at her weak efforts to appear solemn, which was difficult to achieve when she was feeling so joyful she could float, Mr. Tanner dipped his head and raised his brows as though about to impart a confidence.

When he paused, she leaned forward and released her lips to prompt, "Yes? Have you more to add?"

"I love your laugh," he astonished her by saying.

"My laugh? Are you infirm? Have your ears gone on protest? Down to Piccadilly perhaps?"

"My lugs work splendidly, I assure you."

"I laugh like a crone." Or so Father had said once. Letheridge had concurred, casting a rheumy scowl toward his newly intended, enticing Juliet to keep her laughter to herself.

"I think the rusty cackle you free when tickled is charming. Uninhibited. Absolutely adorable, as is the woman behind it."

Blinking away not tears of mirth now but ones of emotion so profound she couldn't fathom how to express it, Juliet only said, "There's been precious little in my life to laugh about until recently."

Very recently, as in once applicant twenty-four prowled into her sitting room and forever took command of her heart.

"Well, I hope you laugh often and loudly," he told her emphatically, as though seeking to convince her of his sincerity. "I find it unfettered and unpretentious, everything I never knew a lady could be and I realize now I cannot imagine my life without the sound."

She scrubbed away any remaining trace of moisture. Her croaky laugh—he *liked* it? "I do believe, sir, that's likely the sweetest compliment anyone's ever paid me."

Mr. Tanner beamed as though she'd given him two bricks of gold. "Then I say you're just now mantling yourself with the correct type of company."

As he spoke, Juliet heard shuffling, a mild disturbance just on the other side of the door. No doubt Wivy must be despairing of her by now, given how long she and her favored applicant had been ensconced.

The slight noise served to return her focus to their express purpose. She needed to conclude the *official* interview. Then, perhaps, if luck and God and Fate were all smiling down on her today, she and Mr. Tanner might be able to veer into some of those more intimate, unofficial regions together. Although, given the proximity and positioning of his spectacularly stript person, she could scarce imagine how much more intimate they might become.

Relieved when the sounds beyond her sitting room abated without anyone interrupting their interlude, Juliet forced her mind back to the remaining item. The letter.

She still needed to know what manner of lover Mr. Tanner was. But when she opened her mouth to concede it was time that he drew up his drawers and commenced reading, that wasn't at all what emerged.

5

AN UNPLANNED ERUPTION

OLIVA WATCHED as the fluffy paw shot out from beneath the sitting room door, tufts of sandy-orange fur protruding from between each razor-sharp claw.

Glad for the distraction from her chaotic thoughts, Olivia told her speeding heart to calm and knelt to rub her index finger across Henry's front leg.

Her hair flopped forward and beads of water dribbled from the tips. Henry swiped his paw over the droplets, the cat's antics bringing forth a shaky smile. *Good for him. The floor could certainly use a thorough mopping.*

Cringing at the strands uncomfortably glued to her neck, she gathered the sodden mass over one shoulder. The smile faded, transforming into a frown at the mess she continued to make —on the floor and of her life.

Because holding a conversation with a cat was preferable to castigating herself or noticing how her drenched dress was plastered to her body, she whispered, "And what exactly do you think they're discussing now, hmm?"

She'd heard enough to surmise things were going well indeed for her friend and employer.

Racing through the rambling manor to the modest room she'd claimed as hers, with the intent to put her hair and person to rights after that unexpectedly glorious (and guilt-inducing) "walk" in the rain, Olivia couldn't resist detouring past Juliet's sitting room.

Now she couldn't seem to leave. Not that she was eavesdropping, the muted rumbles of Mr. Tanner indistinguishable, for the most part. But when Juliet laughed? Now *that* had come through the thick door clear enough. How wonderful to hear and know that sweet, sweet Juliet had finally found someone she could be herself with. Someone who she *wanted* to be with.

Instead of feeling jealous as one might expect of an older, poorer, definitely less creative companion to be, Olivia was in alt on her friend's behalf.

And in awe of herself—and her recent actions.

In awe? Certainly not! She meant dismayed, disappointed even, at what she'd been doing. The subterfuge. The secrets! So completely unlike her.

But oh how it'd been worth it, a tiny part of her acknowledged. So very worth it.

Heavy, rapid thumps coming from the direction of the stairway heralded a new arrival seconds before she heard the corridor-muted shout. "Lady Juliet!"

Giving Henry's paw one last pat, she rose and hastened toward the landing to intercept Jacks. "Shhhh." Olivia motioned toward the sitting room behind her. "We ought not interrupt them, I'm thinking."

"We 'ave visitors," he began, only to break off and exclaim, "By the devil! Miz Hales! Ye... Ye look..."

Self-consciously, Olivia raised both hands to the hank of hair residing over one breast like a waterlogged washcloth. She started to wring out the mass, then stopped when several drops plopped to the floor. "I'm a mess. I know."

"A mess?" Jacks reared back, appraising her from soaked skull to soggy slippers. After noting the muddy streaks trimming the bottom of her once pristine dress, his thoughtful gaze returned to hers. "I'm seein' more than a mess, I could be fergiven fer thinkin'."

Double drat! It was apparent, then? What she'd just done with applicant twenty-five? Mortification poured through her veins like syrup. It was one thing to indulge herself as she had. Another to have someone else discern it!

Thank God the only man *witness* to her crime was gone. Gone for good.

That last thought should have brought a semblance of comfort. It didn't.

Down the hallway, Henry swiped his paw like mad from the other side of the door, a stick of orange fur waving furiously at her to come back and play.

"Wot's up with 'im?"

Relieved Jacks' attention was no longer on her bedraggled person, Olivia promptly answered, "I think he wants out."

"That's seen to easy enough."

When the manservant started to move past her, Olivia halted him with a negative shake of her head. "Nay. The door's locked. I tried a moment ago."

"Locked, ye say?" His surprise, and more importantly obvious satisfaction at what that implied, mirrored her own. "Well, 'Enry can't be wantin' out too bad or 'e'd be yowlin'. 'E's just having a spot o' fun wi' ye."

"Aye." Blowing a mental kiss Henry's direction, Olivia started down the hallway, away from the door. She indicated Jacks should follow. "And locked is how it'll stay until *they* decide to open it."

"'E's the one, ye think? That big Tanner feller?" Hearing Jacks describe anyone as *big* was almost comical. "The one that'll save Lady Juliet from the lonesomes?"

"I do."

Jacks snapped his fingers as if just remembering something. "*I do.* An' that's why I ran up 'ere to fetch 'er. The vicar's 'ere."

"The vicar? Here?"

"Aye. From Duffield. Claims Mr. 'Astings sent 'im over to do a wedding."

"A wedding? So soon?" Goodness, the solicitor had certainly been confident; her mind whirled at how much. "But the banns—"

"That's fer you and 'im to discuss. Me? I'm jus' bringin' the word."

Mr. Hastings was all that was thorough. Olivia had observed that when she accompanied Juliet on her initial excursions to his office at the onset of this marriage scheme. Mr. Hastings had been the one to suggest obtaining references and medical and financial histories from each applicant. It was also his idea to have each man sign a confidentiality waiver-clause so Juliet's identity wasn't compromised. But in the spirit of *being* compromised, it was Juliet who insisted on requiring a letter from each man's mistress.

At the time, Olivia had silently balked at such a brazen request. Well, perhaps not so silently, offering up several stringent protests on the way home. Now, with a bit of hindsight, she completely concurred on the benefits to be gained by securing such a reference.

If Mr. Hastings had arranged for the vicar to come here to conduct a wedding, then a wedding they'd likely have. Only, given how she suspected things were progressing back in the sitting room... "We need to stall him. Downstairs."

"Eh? Fer 'ow long?"

As long as they take.

"Until Mr. Tanner and Juliet emerge—whenever *they* choose to," she told Jacks decisively, her own body still feeling the achy effects of aborted lovemaking. The warm rush of *any* lovemaking. "No one is to interrupt their, ah…the interview."

"Right-o." She swore Jacks winked at her. "An' 'ow do ye want I should stall the man?"

"I'm not certain." She cast about her spinning mind for ideas. "Invite him to dinner. Serve him a scone."

Reaching the top of the stairs, Olivia halted, recalling her state of dress and the need to exchange her drippy garments for dry ones.

In the several weeks they'd resided here, not once had anyone uninvited called upon them. The vicar? *Now* of all times? How she was supposed to compose and conduct herself in front of a holy man of God after the amorous adventures of the afternoon? It didn't bear thinking upon!

Oh but certainly the afternoon did…strong arms, warm lips, the taste of first sunshine and then a male chest…

"...an' the semen...yer dress..."

Her wayward thoughts cartwheeled back to those few stolen moments and distracted her from the current one. Surely she could be forgiven then for not instantly grasping the sentence that now hung heavily, expectantly, in the air.

"Well?" Jacks prompted. "What 'ave ye to say?"

Fine black hairs, sparsely coating muscles so very hard...their texture teasing her palm... "Hmmm?"

"Aurr-hmm!"

Tuned in now to Jacks' frustration at her inattentiveness, Olivia replayed what he'd just said. Or at least she attempted to.

The semen...your dress.

Wha—?

The vague comprehension was enough.

Olivia blanched. Had to put one arm on the wall to keep from crumpling in a swoon. What had he said? "Semen?" she squeaked on a whisper. "*On my dress?*"

Whipping her long skirts this way and that with her free hand, to and fro and up and down with hurried, harried motions, she searched frantically for the condemning evidence.

Jacks cleared his throat. Then cleared it a second time when the first failed to gain her attention.

When he coughed so loudly a third time she was almost knocked off her feet, she halted her frenzied search. Reluctantly looked up. Paling all the more under his knowing gaze, she murmured, "What is it?"

"I *said* that seaman was back too, the navy man, the one from earlier. Come to pay 'is address to ye— I mean to the *lady* of the 'ouse."

"He's here now?"

Jacks grinned as if her express purpose was putting on a grand old show for his exclusive entertainment. And as though he thought she was doing a bang-up job of it. "Aye, an' askin' to see the lady of the 'ouse. Again."

Again. When they both knew *she* was the only female he'd spoken with.

Oh Lord.

Realizing it was a bit late to petition His pardon, especially given how one of His minions currently resided downstairs, Olivia released her hold on the wall and started to slump toward the floor. Given how crumbly the rest of the abode, it wasn't too far off to consider she might literally slink right on through…

Too fast for her own good, Jacks grabbed both her shoulders and steadied her, only easing his grip when she nodded her thanks. He rocked back on his heels. "Yes, indeed. The gent asked fer an 'audience' with yer ladyship, *Lady Olivia*."

Well.

Well.

And wasn't this her afternoon sins coming back to bite her on the arse?

"NO, PLEASE!" Lady Juliet cried in earnest. "Do not cover it—yourself—up. Not quite yet."

Thinking this particular erotic episode had reached its natural conclusion, though certainly not the conclusion his cock envisioned, Zeus had once again bent to retrieve his buckskins from around his knees. Deuced uncomfortable it was, standing there in the nearly altogether as she admired and issued orders while the remainder of her charms remained comfortably—for her—out of sight.

"I'm not finished watching...you," she added softly and sweetly enough only a hardened bounder could refuse.

And Zeus' determination to remain in control melted. A bastard, he might be. But a bounder? Never!

Rising to his full height, he vised his fingers tightly at the root of his excessively exhibited erection, hoping to stem his lingering arousal and forestall any potential embarrassing consequences. "If I'm not hearing further reasons, if I'm not to reorder my clothing, if this interview is not yet at an end"—and he actually hoped it wasn't—"then, pray, what shall I answer next?" Or do next? Because if she didn't issue an order to his liking and soon, Zeus figured his ballocks were about to win out over his brains. He'd be kicking off boots, buckskins and drawers and launching himself toward the settee, her confounded missish hesitations be damned.

"I… I…"

He clenched his staff harder, strove to keep his expression bland. "If you don't want me making the decision for you, you better decide posthaste."

"I wish for you to touch yourself again, as you were doing earlier."

Though his mind rebelled at doing anything more without her *direct* participation, his mouth and body had no such reservations. "Like this?" Ordering his fist to ease the iron grip it'd assumed at the base, he scrolled his circled fingers up his entire length, stunned to see his shaft shaking. His entire arm trembling.

Hoping his voice didn't betray how damn close to the edge the action—or more accurately, *her* obvious appreciation of the action—brought him, Zeus said, "Is this what you wanted?"

Her hushed, "Aye, it is," was all the encouragement his body needed. As though it but lived to do her bidding, his hand languidly stroked over his rod, thundering the storm of desire through him with more ferocity than anything raging outside. Forcing every fiber of his being to luxuriate in the licentious act of performing before her.

The bewildered look of awe and approval taking over her expression, all their talk of licking and wickedness, only expanded his girth, roughened his breath.

"And what else?" he queried, sensing the tightening in his muscles, the imminent release advancing inexorably forward. Zeus ordered his hand to cease moving. It ignored him.

"What else?" he demanded harshly, when she failed to issue another instruction, her gaze now affixed, no wavering evident, upon his flying fist. "Dammit, what else? What other deuced thing would you have me—*Aarrruuuggghhh!*"

The unintelligible sound strangled from his throat as his arm defied every bit of restraint and self-control he sought to enforce upon it. His hand refused to relax its grip. His hips refused to halt their furious thrust and retreat. His dirk refused to stem the tide of its eruption, and Zeus, a grown, experienced man, one who'd *never* previously had any difficulty controlling his body or its urges…well, Zeus watched, distraught, as his crown blasted semen straight into the air. A jetting arc of milky-white that streamed toward his gaping audience but landed shy, painting instead his embarrassment over her tattered rug and the remnants of the dainty tea service and remaining scones still arranged on the table between them.

"Ohhhhhhh-ahhhhh," she exclaimed on a sigh, her wide eyes streaking between his reddened shaft and the *proof* of his impatience.

"Bloody, sodding ballocks!" Zeus cursed, mortification sweeping through him like a tidal wave.

Whipping around, ignoring her cry to remain, he clumsily escaped toward the empty fireplace where he used the damn alluring, infernal stocking to clean himself—though very little evidence remained on his person, the majority of his seed now decorating her sitting room.

After scraping the gossamer silk along his length, unable to control the convulsive twitches of his pelvis or jerks of his cock, his unplanned explosion finally at its end, Zeus growled and wiped his hand clean as well.

Furious with himself, he returned his buckskins and drawers to their rightful place, shoving his disobedient dirk deep in their confines while pointedly ignoring her repeated, somewhat timid entreaties to face her and let her watch—not bloody likely! He was already granting her another splendid view of his white arse! Breath haggard, and with fingers that felt far too swollen and sensitive, he mangled his way up the buttons on either side of the front fall, wrenching one clear off in his haste to get them all fastened.

"Ballocks!" he cursed again, with nothing left to do...save climb over the grate and into the chimney, perhaps? Might not the moldering mortar aid in his quest and grant escape onto the roof? Where the chipped and missing tiles were likely to speed him on his way—to a timely demise. Mayhap then she'd forget his name, his shame, his—

"Mr. Tanner, I order you to present yourself before me!" Evidently she'd reined in her amazement at witnessing his climax, for she now sounded in full possession of her demanding tendencies. Nor had she forgotten his name, devil take her! "Mr. Tanner, it's time you—"

"Nay!" Red-faced and ready to breathe fire—he'd light the one in the hearth himself if he could, singe his bloody breeches on the way up and out!—he spun on his heel but made no effort to move closer. Attempting to mask his humiliation and bluster his way past this impossible impasse, Zeus snarled, "Nay. *You* will not order me to do anything, never again. Though I begin to understand why you wanted a man not noble—so you could lead him around like a pup on a string, lord over him and—"

"'Tis not so! Not even close!" Eyes pleading with him to believe her, she insisted, "I wanted an untitled man so he would *talk* to me, converse *with* me and not simply issue orders and commands *at* me. Order my actions and command my affection where none exists." Her voice turned ragged. "I wanted a man my eyes found appealing and my lips longed to touch, my tongue to taste."

Upon hearing that, his ire softened, annoyance abated.

"Do they?" When all she did was stammer unintelligibly, he took a single step toward her and elucidated. "Do your eyes find me appealing?"

Another slight stutter and then, "Very much so."

"And your lips? Your tongue?" Two more steps.

"Hunger for your taste—just not down there. Not yet."

"'Tis admirable. Amazing, really. A woman, a lady, as forthright as she is adorable. As intriguing as she is vexing." Was it any surprise he'd already succumbed to her bewitching spell? Three more steps brought him to his former position, making his capitulation complete.

“Intriguing? Me?”

Of all he’d said, that’s what she latched on to? “Most assuredly so. Tell me, Lady Scandal, if your affections are not to be commanded, then how are they to be won?”

“Any man named after a god who stands so nobly among my ignoble things, speaking to me with heart and heat and truth, looking as you do, Zeus J. Tanner, well, I confess, my affections are nearly yours to command.”

“Nearly?”

“There is still the matter of a letter you’ve yet to finish.”

The blasted letter? They were back to that? “You still require it to be read? After all that has gone between us?”

She’d be the death of him yet.

“I do. And to completion.” So very primly, so utterly proper, did she order this directive, Zeus no longer knew what to make of her. And after he’d exposed and embarrassed himself beyond what any prideful man would ever consider, did he have it in him to balk further?

Pride may keep you company, but it won't warm you at night. Remember that, Zeus, as you so doggedly pursue your fortune. The prosy phrase intoned on more than one occasion by his dear mama picked such an inopportune time to rear its guidance he could do naught but heed it.

He placed the soiled stocking on the table and bent to retrieve the letter from where it had fallen. As his gaze scanned the crisp vellum, trying to locate his place, he saw not the script inked upon the page but instead the look of wonder upon Lady Juliet's face as she'd watched him earlier, inciting his body's response.

The lassitude that'd stolen over his limbs after the unintended release evaporated, changing into the renewed thrum of desire.

"You may begin."

He jerked his head back to hers. "I'm unsure where I left off."

"'He will set his sights' or thereabouts."

He grunted. "Your memory is excellent."

She glowed under the modest praise. "'Tis a trait I applied myself to develop."

"You honed it well."

As if to confirm the blasted talent, she repeated, "He will set his sights..."

Zeus coughed once into his hand, delaying the inevitable, but eventually he forced out, "He will set his sights upon stroking you to heights of ecstasy before claiming his own. His tongue..."

"Yes? Your tongue...?"

"*His tongue will surely delight you to no end. The agility with which he employs it shall—*" Zeus broke off and sliced his arm through the air, more than ready to rid himself of the damning letter once and for all. The unlit fire beckoned once again—if only it'd been burning! "Was not what I shared earlier sufficient?"

"Are you finished with her words? No, I think not." She answered with so much haughty reserve he wanted to shake her. Then kiss her.

Show her all his "delightful" tongue could do in her mouth and everywhere else.

From her perch upon the settee, she gave him a condescending smile. "Read the remainder, if you please, and stop dallying. How else will I know whether it contains a warning of some sort?"

A warning? Just what was she expecting?

"As to that," she continued earnestly, leaving him flummoxed by the turn of her thoughts, "why have your *former* mistress write your character? Why not your current one?"

"You're not just innocent! You're oblivious to the ways of men and women if you think any man is mutton-headed enough to tell his *current* lover he's seeking another. And for your elucidation," he all but exploded, the burden of passion assuaged just a few moments ago now returned with a vengeance and lending fire to his complaint, "I don't *have* a current mistress. I stopped funding one years ago so I could accumulate my blunt for things more important!"

"What manner of things, if I might ask?"

"You...might...not." Striving for control, he inhaled down to his toes. And almost fell over when the scent of her arousal nearly knocked him to his knees. "I seem to be the one doing all the answering. All the acceding." But he wasn't the only one aching for a true release, not if her increased squirming was anything to judge by. "This conversation is terribly uneven!"

His aggravation didn't faze her. "You *are* the one being interviewed," she pointed out so punctiliously he wanted to throw something.

So he did. He crushed Marianna's asinine reference in his fist and pitched it toward the settee. It bounded off and skidded across the table, coming to rest against a flower-stuffed vase.

They both stared at the rumpled parchment, neither making a move toward it.

"There it is. Read it yourself," he challenged. "I said I was done taking orders. It's time I showed it."

Never taking her gaze from the page, she blinked furiously. "I-I'd prefer you read it to me."

“Well, that’s too jolly bad because I’m done catering to your whims without you answering anything in return.” He looked for his shirt. “And I’ll be damned if I’ll stand around undressed while you sit there all high and mighty, Miss I’m-the-one-doing-the-interviewing-so-what-you-want-matters-not-a-whit!”

“That’s not how I meant it!”

“Oh no?” Zeus craned his neck first one direction then the other, still searching. “You sit on your throne, behind your big, fancy screen, hiding from your applicant peasants, lording over—” Not spying the linen shirt he’d given up too soon and too damn easily, he was starting to realize—too damn late—he rounded on her. “Where in blazes did you stash my shirt?”

“I… I…”

“You *what*? Now that I already performed to request and am no longer your obedient, sycophantic lapdog, you want me to leave? Is that it?”

“No! Not at all. The truth of it is…is…”

"Is what, dammit? Stop staring at the flowers and spit it out! Whatever your tongue's tripping on. The way you're behaving, it's liable to poison you if you don't."

Stricken eyes met his. "I…I cannot read."

6

BORN TO PRIVILEGE…AND NOW PASSION

"Y-YOU…" Words failed him. "*You* cannot read?"

In a trice, his anger drained away and Zeus found himself on the settee beside her, gathering her clenched hands into his own. "But you're aristocracy! Married to an earl!"

"Daughter to a viscount, but there you have it." She manufactured a brave smile. "In my family, reading wasn't judged a necessary accomplishment for a mere female. Unlike embroidery, speaking French, or being accomplished on the pianoforte. Music? I can read the greatest of Haydn's symphonies, but recognizing words beyond my name? My father did not deem it of value. Nor did Lord Letheridge."

Somehow her fingers had turned, twined within his, both his palms cradling one of her hands. Her other, he saw, was tangled in her shift. "But you're a *lady*, born to wealth and privilege."

"I'm a *female*," she stressed, "born to accede to the dictates of men. Now *laisser aller*!" *Let it go*, she pleaded with her eyes as well as her tone.

With a decisive squeeze, Zeus released her hand and seized the despised parchment. Flattening the creases over his thigh, he realized reading the words upon it no longer posed a burden. Instead, they provided an opportunity. A *privilege*. One she'd been unfairly denied.

One he should be grateful for.

She covered his smoothing efforts with one palm. "Nay. You do not have to finish."

He captured her wrist and relocated her hand to his chest—bad decision, that, but once made, one he chose not to retract. “Shhh. I now want to. In light of what you’ve shared, I need to. Now where were we?”

“Your tongue, I believe.” She said it swiftly, pinkening all over.

“Ah, yes. My blighted, delightful tongue.” A deep breath for courage lifted his torso and she flexed her fingers against him. The palm now splayed willingly across his chest burned a path straight to his soul.

Groaning silently at the delicate pressure, Zeus searched for his place. “Tongue…tongue… Ah. Here we are. His tongue shall surely delight you to no end. The agility with which he employs it will curl your toes, warm your heart, and sear you everywhere in between. And his penchant for feet is equally delightful, if rather naughty. But I urge you to let his tongue have its way—in all things. The rewards will be considerable. And finally…”

He faltered a moment when he reached the one line Marianna had composed without giggles accompanying the flourish of her quill. The one line she’d paused over, granting him a bittersweet smile of remembrance before finishing out, both writing and speaking, "*Finally, I can make no greater recommendation for that of trusted friend and lover than the indomitable Zeus J. Tanner. If further details are needed, I remain... Yours, Marianna Longley, Lady Torrington.*"

"Lady?" Juliet's hand tensed upon his skin, tweaking a couple hairs. "She's *married?*"

"Is now. Wasn't then."

Thunder cracked nearby, virtually drowning out her hushed, "Do you care for her still?"

Ahh, definitely an innocent. To exhibit jealousy over so long ago an association. And one gleaned from a reference she required!

"As a friend and no more," he told her sincerely, choosing to omit the details of how he'd rescued the young widow-turned-courtesan, new to plying her dubious trade, from a pair of bosky peers who thought if they had the blunt then she had no say in the matter.

Zeus had used his substantial size and formidable fives to teach them her protests said differently. In return, the gently bred Marianna had schooled him in manners and elocution and the ways of love from a lady's perspective. Now he summarized those several years for Juliet. "She took me under her wing when I was new to London, imparted town bronze and instruction in the ways of women and the world. I, in turn, sheltered her for a time. *Voilà tout.*" *That is all.* "Our romantic liaison has long been extinguished and neither of us pine for its return. And they *aren't* fripperies," he added, pointing to the embroidered screen, "your masterpieces. Not at all."

"You know?" As though wilting in shame, her fingers attempted to slide from his chest. Catching her wrist again, Zeus resisted the impulse to direct them decidedly south, and instead kept them right where they were, snug against his torso.

"What? That you create artistry with *yarn* I assume your clutch-fisted husband refused you? Aye. From what I've seen, along with yourself, your companion Miss Hales, and hairy Henry here..." Zeus raised one leg and pointed to his boot. The tassel swung freely, thanks to the cat's current batting maneuvers. Giving the purring head a chin scratch, Zeus nudged Henry on his way and lowered his foot to the floor. "Your art is the only thing of value inhabiting this rickety tomb. Now I have inquiries to make of you and for every one you avoid answering, I shall remove another article of clothing."

"You will?" Was that excitement in her voice? Or outrage?

"With eagerness and authority."

"My clothing...or yours?"

"It shall be *my* choice. 'Tis time you learned who'll be 'lord' in this household if you take me as husband."

"Very well. Proceed, Zeus J. Tanner. Wait—tell me what the 'J' stands in for?"

She would have to ask that.

After a moment's pause, he gave his standard reply. "James. Now, how many men have you told to shed their shirts?"

"Only one. You." She answered promptly. Too promptly. He'd never get them both naked if this was how she intended to cooperate.

Yet... "Pleased to hear it." Very pleased, in fact. "And how many have you demanded reveal their mistress's letters?"

"You are the first I requested it of."

"Simply making you aware, I plan to be the last. Have you ever been kissed?" She hesitated. Rather than take advantage and start stripping her bare, because he craved hearing the answer, he encouraged, "The truth now."

"Not in such a manner I'd want to repeat the experience."

"Yet you're willing to trade yourself for a rich husband? To, let me see if I can recall this correctly, be an amiable wife ready to bear my children? *Lady*"—it came out an oath—"have you any idea what that entails?"

"I'm trying to ascertain it!" Sharp, determined nails pricked him even as her skin flamed red—every enticing, visible inch. And there were a number of them. "Have I not made it clear? I have tenants to feed. Loyal servants to remunerate!"

"You'd relinquish your freedom for these people? People who were thrust upon you because of an unfortunate marriage?"

"Certainly." Said without any dithering at all, eyes focused straight ahead.

Of course she would. The entirety of her absurd advertisement made sense now. As did the required multiple letters of reference, her skewed questioning, even her desire to see his body. "Do I correctly assume you aim to find pleasure in the marriage bed this go-round?"

She blinked swiftly. "One can dream."

"How did you hurt your leg?"

"I..." Juliet braved meeting his gaze again. Though his rapid-fire interrogation was discomfiting, the heat in his eyes gave her leave to continue. She stared back at his strong, stubborn, still striking-her-to-the-core visage. "I believe I've answered enough of your wretched questions!"

"Do you now?" She'd thought his expression hot before? At her pert response, it blazed. "Did I not warn you of the penalty if you refuse to answer?"

She stiffened her spine. The action served to emphasize her modest breasts, which drew his notice, she saw with no small amount of pleasure. "You did indeed."

"My neckcloth," he rasped, releasing the clamping hold he'd retained on her wrist to haul her onto his lap while taking care not to jostle her injured leg, she noted with awe. "Take it off."

As her hands went to one end of dangling silk, his took hold at her waist, anchoring her securely atop his muscled thighs.

Juliet applied herself to unknotting what remained. Her fingers shook, not because the task was so very foreign but because of how he watched her, his remarkable eyes skimming over her features time and again, their daunting intensity belied by the slight smile quirking one side of his mouth.

His smile grew just before he released his right hand from her waist to brush several stray hairs behind her ear. The job done, his fingers lingered, traced the perimeter of the shell, then meandered down the side of her neck, the pads tapping against her skin in time with the smattering of raindrops that plopped into the upper windowpane and onto the ledge where the lower sash had been propped up to let in the day. Slow…unhurried…unending…

Juliet's breath hitched. The knot was history, as were any pesky doubts. Up close, his spicy-fresh scent was invigorating, his sensual touch and seductive scrutiny intoxicating. Gathering one long end of silk, she leaned forward to unwind it from his neck.

"My cue, I believe," he whispered just before his traveling hand went to her nape and tilted her head. His lips hovered over hers. "Open for me, sweet. I would taste you now."

Her woman's place clenched at his words, her pelvis convulsed forward, but Juliet had no time to question either action, not when he bent his head to claim her mouth.

Zeus, king of the gods. He commanded her submission with no more than a single, unhurried glide of his lips across hers. Twice more he made the journey, then his tongue stroked a horizontal swath across the seam of her lips. Juliet's tongue pressed stiffly against her closed teeth.

His mouth opened over hers, encompassed her lips and drew forth the only possible response —a whimper. Then a sigh. Abandoning the neckcloth, she turned her upper body into his and crushed her breasts to his chest, her palms flattening on the hot skin of his shoulders, fingernails digging into pliable muscle.

His tongue licked again, then he drew back and swore. Wrenching the silk free with two overhead turns of his arm, he rid his neck of the strip and tossed it aside. Snaring her eyes, he ordered, "Tell me why Miss Hales conducted the interview."

Heart pounding madly, she remained resolutely silent.

"I'll unlace your stays." It was a glorious threat.

"Kiss me again." The last syllable barely spoken, his mouth returned, harder this time, with more urgency. Hot and open and beckoning hers to be the same.

His fingers sped along her back, swiftly unlacing her corset while his tongue again quested for entry. Twisting upon his lap now, the ache he caused swirling everywhere, she granted it, parting her lips.

Yet his tongue remained beyond. "You come to me," he demanded. "Give yourself to me else I go no farther."

Though he requested it of her—and in no uncertain terms—Juliet was aware, achingly so, how he was giving her a *choice*. Proceed or not. It was her decision.

At last she'd found him! The one man above all others who met her requirements and exceeded many of them, she thought, almost purring her satisfaction as his male protuberance surged against her—*Zeus*.

Eagerly she braved venturing forth, extending her tongue past his lips and into his mouth, a tiny, triumphant sigh accompanying the action.

Immediately, their tongues met and engaged in a clash of discovery, one that echoed the fervency of his fingers frantic along her spine, deftly unthreading the laces. He sucked her bottom lip into his mouth and worried it with his teeth. She muffled a squeal as sensations streaked through her stomach and thighs.

Against the sensual onslaught, Juliet gasped for air. He gave her his.

A second passed and the pressure upon her ribs eased. Her lungs automatically expanded, taking in more of the life-giving, lust-affirming essence that was Zeus.

Groaning deeply, he tore his mouth from hers in order to work her corset over her head, dragging the stiff boning past distended nipples that hungered for more attention, atop breasts that felt strangely expanded and heavy. "I need...need you..." *Courage, Juliet. Just tell him.* "To massage away these aches you've roused."

ZEUS THREW the contraption to the floor, taking little nips and nibbles of her chin, her neck, working his way down, more than ready to massage away her "aches". Just as soon as he created a few more.

"Why," he gasped, delirious on the taste of her, on the scent of passion rising between them. Her hands were wild upon his chest, nails raking through the hair covering his torso, her unbridled enthusiasm sending riotous vibrations straight to his groin. After nuzzling the inviting curve of one breast, Zeus pulled away and framed her cheeks within his trembling grasp. "Why hide behind the screen? Why hide this lovely body...this precious face?"

Grey eyes glinted. "That's three I refuse..." Defying his fragile hold, she leaned forward and kissed his chest, ran her lips over one pectoral while scoring her nails across the tops of his shoulders, drawing a shudder from his body. "Refuse to answer. Three! Your breeches *off*. I want to see you again. *Need* to see you." Her fingers went to the fall of his buckskins. "Take them off! And your drawers..."

Zeus chuckled. To have a lady—*his* lady—this eager for their marriage bed... Could a man such as he ever want for anything greater?

She scooted back on his thighs and together they wrested his shaft from confinement. At once, her spirited zeal wavered. Silvery eyes flashed from his to the bounty in her hands, and his amusement fled.

Breathing like a stallion after a hard, sweaty ride, Zeus took in the look of wonder on her face, suffered her delicate exploration, and realized—whether this was truly her first time or not—he had a character reference to live up to. Couldn't go blasting off like some unlicked cub.

As you did not an hour ago?

Damn!

While he sought the best way to slow their sexual journey so he didn't reach the finish line before she'd barely left the gate, Lady Juliet renewed her agonizing ministrations, lightly, reverently it seemed, fondling the length of his rod with such curiosity and care she created her own brand of torture. One designed to enrage his body while enthralling his mind.

"Thank God I did spew earlier," he muttered, raking his hair back so he could watch without interference, "to my everlasting shame."

"Hmmm? And why is that?"

Every tentative, tormenting motion of her fingers upon his erection stole more of his typical reserve, else he wouldn't have spoken aloud. Wouldn't have confessed, "Or I'd be in no position to withstand your torture."

"*My* torture?" Posed as though she liked the sound of possessing such an unexpected talent. Emphasizing the torturous power she had over him, she tightened her fingers.

"Aye. Your touch upon my cock feeds my fantasies, fires my blood." His dirk jumped within the renewed, heartier grasp.

"Are they always this thick?"

"They?" He strove to block out the increasing dribbles and drips coming in from the window, spraying the back of the settee. Stinging his bare shoulders. Why did it have to start raining again so hard *now*? When she was caressing him in such a manner?

"Your male protru—"

"My *cock*. Aye, when aroused."

"Leth's was never—"

Thoughts of raindrops drowned in the deluge of jealous and protective urges that seized him. Her words choked off when his fingers clamped on her nape and tipped her head up until their eyes met. "Let us be clear. When you're touching me like this, I don't ever want to hear his name cross your lips, is that understood?"

"Aye." Her hold secure around his poor, beleaguered male protrusion, she blinked up at him. Licked her kiss-plumped lips, then looked back at his crown, straining out between her fingers.

Her mouth. Again, he craved it.

Give her time.

Ah, God. It had been so long since he'd had a woman, longer still since he'd yearned for a *particular* one, or even felt the driving need to claim her mouth, to see her consume him. His shaft disappearing into her hollowed, hallowed depths.

Lady Scandal scandalized his innards to such a degree, his brain couldn't tell up from down, out from in, and his bauble just wanted to blow—

In her hand.

In her mouth.

Goddammit. This wasn't like him.

As if to punish him for his unholy thoughts about such an innocent, the sky chose that moment to further unleash its wrath, the peltering downpour emphasizing the ferocious pounding of his blood. He fisted his hands in her shift where it bunched at her thighs, striving for patience even as he swelled under her stirring attentions. Heart and cock both, lurching uncontrollably in response to this enchanting woman and her unguarded, unassuming manner.

But there was one thing he could control—his need to see her in bed. Upon sultry, satin sheets perhaps. "Why don't we take this interview up to your bedchamber and I'll demonstrate—"

"I regret we cannot." Said so swiftly, she couldn't have given the matter a speck of consideration.

"Forgive me. That was too forward—"

"No! No it wasn't." Her maddening clasp stroked up his shaft again. "You weren't. 'Tis because it leaks that I said no."

"It leaks? Your bedchamber?"

"The roof. After all the rains this past week, my room is soggy beyond reckoning, I'm afraid."

Ah. At the reminder, he did recall how her advertisement had mentioned roof leaks needing repaired. He'd have to see to that sooner rather than later. Make those silk sheets and her satin limbs a reality…

"The settee it is, then."

"Oh, do ask me something else," she said on a wisp of air, her fingers about to send him round the bend—or to straight Bedlam. "Hurry!"

And she called *him* impatient?

Zeus paused, reflecting. There remained so much still to be asked, discussed…*discovered*.

But her breathy encouragement and the lure of tasting her proved too great a temptation. Time enough to tame his mind's curiosity later. For now, he needed to explore the rest of her body —with his own.

"Shall I demonstrate my command of my delightful tongue?" he queried as calmly as possible, in view of how said tongue was practically frothing at the remembered taste of her mouth, at the thought of sampling her intimate charms, those honeyed secrets shielded betwixt her thighs. "I confess a need to do so, to see if *you* find it pleasing as well."

Her stroking fingers skidded to a halt...brow furrowed. "You want to entertain me with witty *repartée*—now?"

Laughing more than any man in his position had a right to—Who knew lovemaking could be so refreshing?—Zeus gingerly lifted her off his lap. Sliding her back onto the settee, he guided her down with a gentle push to her shoulder.

She dug her elbows into the cushion and propped herself upright, indignation firing her gaze. "Where's the humor, pray? For I fear

’tis *me* and my ignorance you find merits mock—”

“No you don’t!” Splaying her resisting arms wide so he could lean forward and steal a kiss —then slowly steal his way toward her breasts, Zeus chided, “Don’t turn stiff on me now.”

Tugging the shift out of his way, he winced when several threads snapped, but he didn’t stop, not until one finger tapped upon a bare nipple.

“But—” Eyelids fluttering, her protests dwindled as the tiny nub grew taut, firm beneath his touch. “But…”

“Show some trust, my lady. Trust that I know what I’m doing. You owe me that, wouldn’t you say?” Rotating his thumb over the beaded tip, he held her gaze. “Have I not answered every blasted question you’ve lobbed my way? Allowed my pride to be shredded fulfilling your bedeviling requirements? Suffered Hastings’ judgment, that of Miss Hales’, and ultimately your own? Choked down a scone not fit for starving swine?”

“What?”

Overriding her confused murmur, he demanded, "Did I not disrobe without demure—"

"Hardly without demure!" Despite her rejoinder, her mild pout at his litany of valid complaints, her back arched, thrusting her entire breast toward him.

"Very good, my lady."

"What is?" she grumped, her diffident gaze bouncing from her distended nipple to his chest to a point somewhere over his head. "That I weakly allow myself to be mocked?"

"Nay, never that." He settled his broad palm across the pliable mound of her breast, and damned if the firm tissue didn't leap into his touch as if it belonged there.

"That I'm too curious to learn what else you may show me I fail to depend upon pride to see me strong and instead..." Once again, she cut her gaze to his. "Instead I begin to depend on you?"

"Mayhap I find the idea of you depending upon me satisfying in the extreme." Exhaling audibly with a measure of contentment he'd never thought to feel today of all days, Zeus ensured her splinted leg was fully supported, then he angled the other to hang off the settee, widening her thighs. He climbed into the vee he'd created between those pale, creamy limbs, a broad smile lifting his cheeks. A moment later it was wiped clear when his tongue sought the destination his hand had claimed seconds ago—her plump little breast.

"Mr. Tanner!" she gasp-moaned.

He hollowed his cheeks and sucked sharply, allowing his tongue to bedevil the knot of nipple now held snugly between his teeth.

"Mr. Tanner..."

This time it was a sigh. One of capitulation, of complete and utter sexual surrender. And Zeus couldn't have been more pleased.

Until she added, more than a little primly for their current circumstances and his liking, "My body may melt under your torrid tutelage, but I have yet to be granted an accounting of precisely *why* you deem it necessary to laugh at me."

To punish her for thinking so—especially when his mouth was so very *delightfully* occupied, Zeus drew deeply on her flesh, taking all he could inside the hot cavern of his mouth. He lashed at the tip of her breast with his tongue. “You horrid, haughty man,” she accused, winding her fingers through his hair, “to do such wicked things...and so splendidly!”

Grinning inside, from ears to erection, Zeus glanced up. While entertaining his eyes with her flushed and piqued features, his mouth with her breast, and his mind with all the bawdy bedchamber antics they’d share in years to come, he stript to skin. Blindly, he rid himself of his boots—nearly wrenching his ankles off in his haste—then he ripped clear through one of his woolen stockings until they too were gone and he could finally dispense with his drawers and banish his buckskins to the floor.

“What is the jest, you wonder?” He spoke around her nipple, doing his best to distract her, unwilling to confess it was her naïveté he found so heartening, so joyful. Worried she might not see those qualities the same way he did. “That a man such as I could find exactly what he's been searching for all his life, and so very close to home."

"I do not—" When he bundled her shift out of the way and brought one hand to the juncture of her thighs, she broke off. When he caressed upward between her open legs, touching her honeyed center, she gasped and came up off the settee. "Do not take your meaning."

After another sweep of his fingers through her damp curls, another sharp pull on her breast, he released the succulent treat and rimmed the puckered areola with his tongue before pledging, "You shall, and soon. Of that I promise." Her womanly scent continued to entice him downward, beckoning him to take further liberties.

Answering the call, his moistened fingertips parted the swollen folds. Her damp heat coated his wandering fingers. Captured him completely. "Have you any doubts, my lady? If so, you'd best speak them now."

He meant about marrying him, because in truth, if he tasted her beyond what he'd done so far, she *would* be his wife.

So when she answered, "Nay, no doubts, Zeus. I want you to show me passion. Every bit of it," using his name, he knew she'd be his forever. That they'd miraculously captured each other.

"But show me your form first," she challenged when he pressed deeper toward her core. "Now that you're fully revealed."

Realizing his exploring fingers had gone a little too far too quickly, Zeus tamped down his own urges and ordered his passion-coated fingers to retreat. Coiling them into a fist, he hiked off her.

"Stay close," she said when he started to step back.

"Did you not see enough earlier?"

"Nay." Then softer, "I may never see enough."

So he halted at the edge of the settee, her heartfelt sigh caressing his ears. Rather pleased with his new position, he stared at one of her dainty feet, the one sans splint and bindings, while giving her time to admire him (he hoped).

Zeus found himself grinning. Even her toes were ladylike.

He swore he could feel her gaze drift along his nude body like a tangible touch. Her silent perusal continued until the tension stretched taut between them.

In his bid to grant her as much time as she needed, Zeus sought a distraction and found one fortuitously close by. Lifting her uninjured foot with his open hand, he cradled it and bent to feather light kisses over her toes. When a tentative swipe of his tongue caused her to squirm, knowing there'd be plenty of time for more attention here *after* they said their vows, Zeus moved on, applying himself to licking a decisive path over the top of her foot, past her trim ankle, over her knee, and up to her thigh where the hem of her shift bumped his nose.

God, he had to taste her. Freely—without any encumbrance between them. "By God, woman, I hope you've seen enough because my patience is—"

"About to be rewarded. Come back."

As he replaced her foot on the cushion, with a damnable arm that shook he couldn't help but notice, Zeus marveled at the set of circumstances that had landed him here, within reach of everything he'd never known he needed. Feeling lighter inside than any man had a right to, he climbed onto the settee between her legs, flattered by her shy, somehow sultry smile. Welcomed by her outstretched arms. "Miss me?"

"You and everything you're teaching me." After that admission, she *mmm'd* her approval when he snugged his groin at her mons. On top of the shift.

Zeus fingered the filmy cotton—the only item of clothing yet to be discarded—and met her inquisitive eyes, scouring his mind for another question she could refuse to answer. "Why did you not learn to read after Letheridge kicked off?"

It was the wrong thing to ask.

"I meant to—truly, I did!" she stammered, frowning and shoving him away in an effort to sit upright.

Zeus knew he'd inadvertently found her Achilles. Dammit, why couldn't he have just continued *kissing* her ankle and kept his chops shut?

Not permitting her to gain distance from him, Zeus kept his heavy body anchored over hers. He attempted to soothe the legs that'd tensed beneath him, unfurling the fist full of her nectar he'd gathered like a prize so he could graze one slickened finger over her thighs. Her scent nearly did him in. "Never mind that now—"

"I did! It's just that with the funeral and his creditors flooding in before his corpse was cold and then the fire that—"

"Shhhh, it's over now." Zeus stilled his foray, endeavored to do the same with her rising panic. "I'll take care of the creditors. Put your mind at rest on that front."

She clutched at his arms as though she was sinking in quicksand and trusted him to pull her out. "But I meant to, I did! Everything changed so precipitously after the house burnt, and—and—"

"Tell me of it, sweetheart. What fire?" Mayhap if she unburdened the words tripping her tongue, they could return to setting her settee on fire with their own carnal conflagration. "What burnt?"

She hugged him closer, pulling him down and burrowing her face into his neck. "'Twas such a tragic loss." She sniffed. "Amherst was so very lovely, my favorite of all his properties."

Her words doused him with ice. "*Amherst?*" Zeus went rigid, saying it. Then he sought comfort by wrapping both arms around her and squeezing her tighter, settling himself more deeply against her. "Amherst?" he whispered hoarsely. "It's...gone?"

7

ENDEARMENTS, CONFESSIONS & COMPLETION

THE NOD of her silky head against the underside of his chin confirmed the worst. "Up in billowing clouds of black smoke that smoldered for days." She turned her face to his, pushed on his shoulders until she could snare his gaze. "Why? Do you know it?"

"I…" He…*what*? What could he tell her? That his reason for being there no longer existed? That his sole ambition these last years was gone? Turned to nothing more than dusty embers blown into oblivion by the first gust of wind.

Then why, he pondered as he stared into her grief-shadowed eyes, then lower at her lips, parted and plumped by his kisses, did it not feel as though his very dreams followed the scattered ash? Why was he not, even now, retreating from her in a fury? Striding quickly away while he cursed the time wasted? The loss of the ultimate goal that had guided his every action for over a decade?

He should leave, allow her the opportunity to marry a better man than he. Maybe that seafaring one she'd sent on his way. A man not consumed with seeking vengeance against a father long dead.

But he couldn't make his feet move toward the door. Couldn't stop himself from brushing his fingers over the tousled strands of red-gold framing her concerned face. Couldn't stop his thighs from wedging themselves more solidly along hers.

"Mr. Tanner?" Her searching fingers feathered over his jaw. "Zeus? What is it? What has you looking so lost?"

Did he tell her? Admit the lure, until meeting her, was not the bounty she offered—that of herself—but lands he not only coveted but loathed? Or did he stay mute? Give her the taste of passion—just a taste, mind—she craved, and then leave, as a true "gentleman" should?

Zeus swore harshly. A true gentleman wouldn't consider tasting anything beyond what he'd already stolen. He'd settle for licking his fingers clean on the way out and never look back.

Well, hell. As though defying his very thoughts, those bound-to-be-tasty fingers opened and after smearing her essence across his chest, rose to entrench themselves against her scalp. And why shouldn't they? A *real* gentleman would never have compromised her to this state to begin with.

Guilt crashed down on him.

A bastard might, by some miraculous stroke of fortune, marry a lady, but that wouldn't change his stripes. Wouldn't make a gallant gentleman out of a churlish cur's seed.

Before he could rationalize it further, mayhap talk himself out of the altruistic action, Zeus wrenched his head from her comforting hold and blurted, "Forgive me, my lady. I must go."

He angled backward, distancing his torso from hers, determined to leave, *to do right*. "I cannot marry you!"

Nails pierced the skin of his shoulders even as she wound her strong leg around both of his. "No! What are you saying? Leaving? You cannot—"

"I came here for Amherst, not for you." The weight of regret made him nearly shout at her. "I don't deserve you!"

"Don't deserve…?" It was a ragged sigh. But her leg only gripped him tighter, the heat of their melded bare skin burning a path to his soul, forcing the confession to erupt like steam trapped too long.

"I'm Letheridge's bastard! *His* damnable son!" And with that admission, though he'd once sworn he'd make any sacrifice, surrender anything necessary to regain his questionable birthright, Zeus realized he wasn't willing to heap more lies upon the ones already uttered, wasn't willing to sacrifice *Juliet*. Wouldn't use additional duplicity nor her own inexperience to do it. "You deserve someone better! Someone forthright. Someone…else."

"Leth's...boy?" Said as though simply the act of comprehending his statement took great strength.

"His *bastard*." Zeus nearly spat at her, making it clear as shattered crystal. He would have no more falsehoods between them.

He expected her to throw him off, to scurry away. To curse him for the deceitful, deceptive rogue he was.

Zeus was confident he'd get over losing her. In another decade. Or ten.

But instead of screeching at him to remove his filthy person from her sight and her life, Juliet wound her arms savagely round his neck. Nearly cut off his air.

But who needed to breathe when she hadn't cast him out? At least not yet...

Zeus clutched her as fiercely as he could. And prayed. For the fortitude to leave or for her forgiveness to stay, he knew not which.

. . .

He couldn't go! Juliet's mind screamed. Not this beautiful man with his impertinently insightful replies.

Discounting the wretch who caught her out due to an untimely dust mote and resulting sneeze, not a single one of the other applicants had seen through the ruse. No one had surmised she watched from beyond the shielded corner, once she'd had the forethought to retreat there after the Mongrel Misadventure.

None of them had realized *she* created the crewel-worked "masterpiece", save Mr. Tanner. While some had told her the truth during questioning and not simply what they thought she wanted to hear, none had done so with his aplomb. With confidence bordering on arrogance.

And certainly none drew her like a magnet, their very person energizing hers in such a way that when she neared them, parts of her came alive for the very first time *in* her life.

And now he sought to desert her? Over nothing more than *his* unfortunate circumstance of birth? "Nay, you cannot! Not if that is your only reason for thinking to do so."

"But Lecherous Letheridge..." She thought he mumbled *rotten, hateful father* and *hated, useless son*. Then clearly, "I should go. Must go. For you. For—"

"No!" She planted hungry kisses on his mouth to still the ongoing protests. Then over his cheek, his ear. "I don't care! It does not matter who sired you! Not to me."

He'd gone rigid as marble above her.

She couldn't stop touching him, brushing her lips across his stubbled jaw. "You're better than all of them, *all of them* I say."

When he attempted to pull away again, she shrilled, "Applicant number six *smoked* here. In my sitting room! After I expressly asked him not to."

"Stave off tempting me, woman!" He hurled the words at her, glaring fiercely.

Juliet glared right back. "Then don't entertain the notion of abandoning me!"

“Ah, God,” he said hoarsely. “Do you not see? Another man would have more experience with crops and sheep, with—”

The only thing she saw was how empty and barren the future stretched out before her if he wasn’t in it. Zeus James Tanner. No one else could be as perfect for her as he. And Juliet was determined to prove it. “Brute twelve spilled copious amounts of tea down his cravat and didn’t even notice!”

“Juliet…” Zeus dropped his head to her shoulder, and she sensed him weakening.

“He did! Drank like a gluttonous goat!”

“No surprise there,” he muttered against her neck, “if you fed him those briny scones of torture!”

That was the second or third time he’d mentioned such a thing.

From beneath his solid presence, Juliet extended one arm and snatched a bite from a scone populating the bottom of the tray. A couple of the ones above it sported “icing” from Zeus’ fascinating, earthy display earlier.

Nibbling, she forced herself to shrug beneath the strangely tantalizing weight of his limbs tangled with hers. “Hmmm. It is rather salty.”

“Salty?” A swift jerk of his head and he saw what she was doing. “Confound it! You can’t eat that!”

She rubbed the bottom of her foot over his leg in a calming gesture. “Whyever not?”

“I...” Staring at the tray, he blanched. When he again tried to scoot off, she coiled her leg between his and dug her toenails into whatever flesh they found. Zeus gave a grunt and met her gaze. “I peaked earlier.” He sliced his eyes toward the table. “Over there.”

“I know you did.” She beamed at him. “And I peeked at you too. More than peeked, I’d say—”

“*Peaked*,” he stressed, paling further. “Spewed, spent. Fired in the air.”

Though she had a substantial inkling of what he referred to, hearing him “spew” such eloquent, earthy vocabulary (and thereby expanding her own), was too enlightening an opportunity to pass up. “Fired what in the air?”

she asked with suitable bafflement. "I've neither seen nor heard a firearm to—"

"Not bullets, devil take me!" He was having a devil of a time of it, that was clear.

"Then what?" she asked helpfully. Or wickedly, depending upon how one wanted to view it.

"Discharged my chitty," he strangled out, the tendons in his neck standing out starkly. "Fetched my own mettle. Spewed my spunk. Jetted my juice!" At that, she had a most difficult task maintaining her bewildered façade. "Do you not behold what's before you?" With a harsh gesture, he pointed to the tray. "The trajectory of the evidence?"

"Evidence? Oh!" she exclaimed with great feeling. "You mean when you..."

"By God, *yes*, that is what I mean." He stole the remaining crumb from her unresisting fingers and tossed it overhead.

"By damn, you cannot *eat* that! I forbid it." The poor dear looked so aghast at the very notion, was so caught up in protecting her supposedly delicate sensibilities, he failed to notice when Henry came round the settee, batting the morsel between his front legs. "And pardon my damn language!"

"Mrrr*owww*." They both looked over to see her precious, if somewhat scraggly, tom bathing one paw as if he'd just downed dinner.

Or one very savory scone.

She chose not to point out the significance to her intended. *Her intended.* How wondrous that sounded, how magical it felt. For by now, Juliet was fair convinced not only were they betrothed, they were bound for life.

To distract him, she pointed to a remnant still on the tray. "Your—ah, the evidence, *you* soaked in here, I believe. Not the piece I tried. See? This, um, darker, moister-looking section over—"

"God grant me patience!" He had the temerity to interrupt her consoling efforts.

"That won't work, you know."

"What won't?"

"Praying for patience. God is busy tending to sinners, I'm sure. And you, dear sir, are a saint.

A saint among men." Twenty-four men at the very least. "Or did you forget?"

"We agreed I *wasn't* a saint. Didn't we? Of course we did!" he finished on a roar.

"Well, pish-posh. Appears I forgot. You do that to me, you know. Scramble my wits. Make me forget everything but you."

"As flattering as that sounds, I'm not convinced that isn't to your detriment. I mean look—" Again he slashed one arm toward the table. "You…just…ate…"

"And watch," Juliet said tartly as she deliberately reached for the darker, moistened section, determined to snaffle *his* wits until he agreed to stay. "I'll do it again!"

Before he could stop her, she popped another brittle piece on her tongue. She chewed and swallowed in a rush. "Oh dear. Appears we ran out of sugar and butter again."

Zeus lifted his gaze to the ceiling. "Is this penance, God? Are you punishing me—"

"Nay, not penance. 'Tis passion," Juliet told him, blatantly licking his bulging arm muscles to rid her mouth of the sorry scone. "Now you, blessed man, taste intriguing." She licked him again, swirling her tongue over the surprisingly silky skin, dazed at not only her desire to do so, but at how she felt no qualms instigating the action. "Inviting even."

He slowly brought his head down to glower at her. "I can't decide whether you'll be the death of me. Or the life." He jerked a nod toward the scattered contents on the tray, that rakish sweep of hair falling forward. "Out of sugar and butter again? *That's* all you have to say?"

She gave a silent nod, choosing to stop—for now—baiting him. He seemed sufficiently snaffled.

"And you weren't apprised of it?"

"The staff keeps trying to protect me from how bad off things are."

NO WONDER she in turn sought to protect them. Zeus marveled at such loyalty—and how it was reciprocated. On the streets, a man would as soon thrust a knife in one's gullet as remain loyal. Especially with meager pay and minimal rations—the very circumstances he knew her servants had operated under for some time now.

Juliet. *Juliet.* "Juliet." Her unexpected acceptance, the way she brushed back his hair, lingering to stroke his jaw, promised to wash away his guilt, every bit as much as the roaring rain buffeting the windows.

"They don't want me worrying."

Neither did he.

But if he wasn't there to protect her, who would? Could he trust another man to always have her interests at heart?

Zeus told his fingers to stop twining themselves within her mussed hair.

"But that matters not," she maintained. "That test was supposed to be a study of your manners. Not of your stomach's resilience. What matters is you hated that dreadful scone! Yet you ate it, with a smile I might add, for *me*."

She was right. By the time the salty silt crossed his lips, he'd been solely focused on pleasing the enchantress behind the screen. He'd no longer been thinking of Amherst.

One rebellious hand traveled toward a creamy breast. Unable to stop himself, he settled his palm over the mound. "Juliet... My lady..."

"Why would you do that"—she gasped when he kneaded—"if not to please me? Because no matter your parentage, Zeus James Tanner, you're *Quality*!"

His mouth and mind were fighting a losing battle. As was his hand which only fondled her more intently. With each desperate word she uttered, she drew him toward her every bit as much as her fingers clasping his cheeks and compelling him to hold her gaze. Every bit as much as her bare foot grazing the back of his thigh, soothing the spot she'd gouged earlier. "Quality? I'm not even—"

"Because you're honest and true!" An elongated clap of thunder loudly proclaimed how she had the right of it. "You make me laugh 'til my throat aches."

When he only shook his head against her restraining hold, as if sensing his disintegrating resolve, she boasted, "Number nine broke my leg!"

His hand froze atop her breast. "What?"

"It's why I had to postpone the remaining interviews. The rotter insisted on bringing his hunting dogs inside. I insisted they be leashed. And *they* insisted on tangling round my legs when Henry insisted they weren't welcome."

His chuckle dried up before it ever emerged. She was so very strong. So damn determined to convince him. When he should be the one convincing her. "Juliet, you're everything sweet and proper and…I'm everything not." He watched his weak-willed thumb draw a circle around her apricot nipple even as he put forth one more attempt to persuade her (and maybe his former self?) how very unworthy he was. "My mother was a maid in his household. Letheridge's. Seduced by the lecher and cast out when his third wife couldn't stomach having his bastard underfoot."

She touched his lips, traced them, seduced him to stop. "Zeus—"

But he wasn't finished. Had to get it all out. "After eight years running free over Amherst, thriving within its walls and on its lands despite his neglect, Mum and I were evicted with only a pittance to salve his conscience—and she with no character or way to find work. I always thought it ironic justice none of his other children lived past infancy. Now I hear myself say that and I realize how cruel and selfish I sound. How just like him."

"You're nothing like him. After three years of hiding my true self, I've blossomed more this afternoon than I have my entire life. Whatever thoughts you had, they're in the past now. Let them trouble you no further."

Oh, the vengeance he'd thought to exact, honing his skills in order to decimate his own father at the gaming tables only to have the old lout stop frequenting London and his clubs just when Zeus amassed enough blunt to bribe his way in. The hate he'd felt, thrived on at the time… It faded now at the compassionate way she continued to gaze up at him—waiting for the rest without judging. Only accepting. "Do you know I came to him five years ago, contacted him through Hastings because he refused to acknowledge me otherwise? Swallowed my self-respect and attempted reconciliation with the ogre who'd cared not whether we lived or died."

His voice broke on the last word. But rather than feeling shame over the weakness, the way she continued to pet him, to console and encourage, gave him strength.

With her in his arms, he'd faced down his demons. Admitted them out loud. And the world hadn't come crashing down.

Instead, Juliet lifted him up.

"Mr. Hastings knows the truth?" she asked lightly.

"Of my origins, you mean? He does. And I'm convinced when I presented myself in response to your advertisement, he scoured my references all the more for it." Her body squirmed a bit beneath his. Zeus ceased torturing her nipple and came onto his elbows, taking more of his weight. Her leg prevented him from going far. "But I was determined to win your lands, never once giving thought to *you*, to what you'd suffered at Lecherous' hands or how my tainted lineage might affect—"

"Stop it, my love." And if that unexpected endearment didn't halt his very blood. Love? "Do you hear yourself? I cared not to condemn your birth before and I refuse to condemn it now. You are the finest man I've met, certainly the only one I could consider taking as husband."

"Juliet—" She slapped his flank to still the protest.

"Do you *want* to stay? Do you want to rebuild Amherst together? With...me?" she finished with the strongest hint of uncertainty he'd heard since she'd confessed her inability to read. When he made no move to abandon his position, she continued with more confidence. "We could, I do believe, hire stewards to oversee these other dilapidated estates, focus *our* efforts there...?"

At her unforeseen but wholly workable suggestion, his blood resumed pumping with a vengeance. Zeus' mind whirled faster than the wind buffeting the sagging rooftop, fiercer than the nails digging into one side of his arse.

That's why Hastings had confined him to Duffield? The crafty solicitor hadn't wanted him discovering Amherst was gone because... He'd been on Zeus' side all along!

Rebuild Amherst...together. How that beckoned. He had the funds, surely. "And we could bedeck it with your magnificent embroideries," Zeus pondered aloud.

To start anew, to start fresh...

But she wasn't finished, not yet. As her splayed palm worked its way over his heated hindquarters, she informed him, "Applicant twenty-three tried to strike Wivy!"

So that was why the prizefighter of a footman had pounded and pummeled the last candidate on the way out? "And was repaid in kind from what I saw," Zeus complimented. Exceptional servants were difficult to come by. Nice to know she already had them in place.

He played his last card; she'd trumped all the others. After nuzzling her downy cheek with his bristly one, Zeus pulled back to gauge her response. "But I lied to you, my sweet, I lied..."

Her eyes narrowed and another slap landed on his backside. Instinctively, he surged against her. "About?"

Heat searing his insides, he confessed. Or tried to. "My middle name. It's not James. It's..."

Hell, this part might be the toughest of all.

"Y-e-s-s-s?"

"It's... Damn me, it's Jupiter."

She strangled off a snort and bit down on the smile that threatened, her face a study of bland inquiry that didn't fool him for a minute. "Ah, interesting. Is that all?"

"Is that not enough? I'm *Zeus Jupiter*, for God's sake!" Unable to withstand her merriment at what he'd never shared with another, he ducked and began plying her pale skin with kisses. "Mum couldn't decide which of the ancient versions—Greek or Roman—were most exalted. So she chose both, by damn."

"And I cannot read even one word of your grand mythological adventures," she imparted on a rusty laugh, sweeping her nails along his back and buttocks, "so I'd say we're well-suited!"

"We are indeed." Rising up, he captured her mouth, allowing his kiss to convey everything he couldn't yet articulate.

Merrowing his satisfaction, Henry used his bare butt as a launch to the back of the settee, causing them both to break apart and smile. Zeus dragged his thumb over her reddened lips, the bottom one slick from his kisses. "I'll teach you, you know. To read."

"You will?"

"With the patience of a saint. But we've another lesson to finish now. One you charged me with earlier—that of showing you passion." Her eyes glinted, then somehow found a spot beyond his left ear fascinating. "And you might as well know, I take my assignments seriously."

"Assignments? That's how you view me? What I've become?" And suddenly she became all soft hesitance.

"Nay, not *you*. But helping you, aye. As in teaching you to read. As in rebuilding Amherst. *Together.*" He offered the commitment, and by association, himself, sincerely. “As in teaching you all about *my* protrusions and paraphernalia, so you have no need to ever again inquire about another’s. About—”

“As if I would!”

“About how well I’m going to love you.”

“Ahhhh.” Her gaze flicked back to his. “And how do you propose to go about something so very challenging?”

With alacrity! “Touch yourself.”

When she stared at him blankly, Zeus angled to the side and pressed his buttocks into the back of the settee to give her maneuvering room, unintentionally squishing Henry’s tail. With a sniff, the cat jumped down.

Zeus breathed a tad easier. It wasn’t necessarily that he minded an audience—Juliet’s earlier amorous appreciation had shown him that—but with the cat out of sight (and hopefully his hindquarters out of claw range) he could finally get back to the business of loving his bride-to-be.

Indicating her cleft by skimming the pads of his fingers over the sunset curls he doubted had ever, before now, seen the light of day, he again instructed, “Touch yourself for me.”

“Umm, pray, *where* exactly?”

“Where might you think?”

“Here?” Obviously stalling, the tide of red sweeping across her features telling the tale more clearly than any loquacious bard, she slipped one hand between them and pinpointed her index finger on the very tip of her sniffer.

“J-u-l-i-e-t.” He spoke as deeply as he could, drawing her name out with grave intensity.

“Z…eu….eu…us…s…s.” The little minx matched him, in timbre and tone.

Snagging that impudent finger perched atop her nose, he attempted to draw it lower. “You know I mean your quim.”

“Touch my…?” The adorable baggage beneath him sputtered. She resisted, rebelled. And judging by the unholy light in her eyes, damn near howled in horror.

"Come now—"

"Zeus! You— I cannot!" The hand he loosely guided downward balled into a lead weight and refused to budge beyond her navel. "A lady *never*— She absolutely never!" The man above her choked on his own laughter. "'Tis not funny!"

"Aye, it is. From my vantage point, absurdly so." He released her straining arm and settled in beside her. He even refrained from freeing a sigh when the marmalade purr bucket hopped up behind him once again.

She must've seen it in his expression though. Wrinkling her recently emphasized nose, she apologized, "He thinks you're usurping his position. As my champion." A quick swish of a fluffy tail confirmed she had the right of it. "He'll learn to share me. He likes you, I can tell."

But Zeus refused to be distracted. A man on a mission, he plowed straight ahead. "A *lady* courageous enough to advertise for a husband, to forfeit clothing and exchange kisses for a taste of passion can do anything she damn well pleases." He let that sink in. Then he added,

"Especially when her chosen husband requests it of her."

As if daring her to deny his assertion, he raised her shift to her waist. Exposing her charms completely. "Now, my lady, touch yourself. No more balking, hmm?"

Mayhap I'd rather touch *you*.

The naughty thought took Juliet by surprise.

Mutinously, determined not to give in to his demand, at least not quite yet, Juliet remained motionless. Henry just gave her a single slow blink—of chastisement?—and jumped down when the wind blew in a few errant raindrops.

Traitor.

To Zeus, she said, "I should call you a brute, a beast."

"You should've called Jacks," Zeus chided, heaving a sigh. He came onto his knees, one on either side of her torso. "Called him long, long ago, and had me tossed out on my ear."

"But I like your ears." And that wasn't all Juliet liked, she knew, given how she couldn't take her eyes off the sight of Zeus' erection. From the way he'd just knelt above her, the thick column swung heavily between them. So close she could reach out and touch it.

So she decided to, swallowing her apprehension, easing her arm forward ever so slowly. And in so doing, received an unexpected boon—avoiding that *other* place he'd requested.

Touch *herself*? Down *there*? Really! The bossy, beastly brute forgot himself.

Ladies hardly dallied and rarely explored skin typically blanketed by garments even during bathing. And that was under the cover of night and night rail! How could she fathom delving deep and discovering her own intimate parts—and in front of him no less?

"My lady?" His upper body was bowed, the corded muscles of his stomach rippling invitingly as he hunkered lower to look into her eyes. "Lady Juliet?"

She noticed how his voice had gone all raspy. His breathing all ragged.

She noticed more the unfamiliar weight of his glorious...prominence, brushing the backs of several fingers once she'd extended her hand.

A sharp flash of white illuminated the window side of him above her, bringing home how dark the sky and evening had grown. But more than that, it highlighted his nude thighs surrounding her. And how her hands had moved to either side and now rested firmly, solidly on each.

His strong muscles shivered beneath her untutored caress. His legs. His *thighs*.

No longer was she simply thinking or saying the taboo words designating his manly form. She was touching him, her virgin fingers mapping the warmly textured territory he'd only recently bared to her avid gaze.

Had that been just this afternoon? Then how was it that it seemed so long ago? As though she'd been yearning to clamp her fingers on these powerful legs forever?

Seeing the bare, usually gloved, hands that she knew belonged to her traversing over not marble but pliable, heated, *flexing* muscle brought home how very far she'd come in such a short time. All thanks to the man above her.

With a resounding hiss and crackle, lightning spiked in her periphery.

"Juliet..." The husky sound of his plea was answered by the dip in her stomach, by the outstretched arms that refused to lower.

The thunderous rumble that crashed outside didn't faze either of them.

She was too busy scraping her palms up the coarsely soft hairs on his thighs and over the smooth, pale skin of his hips...

"Oh God." And poor Zeus, he looked as though he was occupied trying not to keel over. "Are you...? Saints be praised, are you...about to intentionally touch my dirk?"

The undeniable pleading in his hoarse whisper encouraged her onward.

"I believe I am..." Juliet answered the question she wasn't sure Zeus knew he'd asked out loud, given his stunned expression when she anchored her fingers deeper into his muscles instead of shying away.

The slight trembling of his legs as he straddled around her gave her the temerity to continue, loosening her grip on his thighs. She was startled when Zeus moaned, “Oh, God. Stop licking your lips like that.”

Stilling the involuntary motion of her tongue, she slowly inched her fingertips higher, furrowed them through the dense golden hairs at his groin. She stopped just before reaching his…cock. She thought it. Then she said it. “Your cock.”

“Oh, God. Juliet!” Shifting, he clenched his jaw, grasped his shaft in one hand, and fell forward on the opposite arm, bringing the reddened tip closer to her face. Closer to her lips.

“Could you?” he rasped. “Would you?”

It appeared so, because Juliet found her curiosity and desire to please him, as he’d pleased her in countless ways today, overrode inbred caution. Overruled years of repression.

“You don’t have to,” he said swiftly when she made no move toward him.

How could he know observing him from afar was vastly different from seeing him up close, where the heat of his body nearly poured off his skin, the searing allure of his erection simmering between them? Where the single sparkle of fluid emerging from the slit fascinated and entranced? She caught herself and just barely avoided licking her lips again.

But she'd waited too long.

On a harsh exhalation, he edged back. "I can wait. I did promise you patience."

"You did." She slid her hand around one hard thigh and tugged him forward.

"My lady? I meant it. You do not—"

"I now want to," Juliet said, repeating what he'd told her about reading his character. "Need to, I am thinking."

ZEUS WATCHED, awash in amazement, as she took the clear drop from his slit and wiped it across the upper swell of one breast. Her dainty hand returned and she closed it over his own white-knuckled death grip.

Both of them holding tightly to his dirk—his arm quivering and fingers cramping from the restraint he exuded, hers resting lightly on top—she brought him to her mouth.

Where she kissed him!

Placed the puckered bow of her lips to his crown with a barely audible *smack*.

Just when he wanted to howl, to bellow his dismay and disappointment for he'd been dreaming of so much more than a chaste kiss, she opened her mouth and her tongue made an appearance.

Zeus stopped breathing.

Hesitant at first, only an infinitesimal swipe. Then her tongue returned, licked again. Just the very top. Then the side. And once more, that tiny pink temptation leaving a path of wetness down the entire shaft exposed above their joined hands.

And then—thank God Almighty—a circular swipe round the crown that had his lungs remembering to inhale on a gusty intake of air.

A subtle *mmm* emerged from her throat, the exact meaning he couldn't decipher, but the intent clear enough.

Especially when she dug her fingernails in one buttock and urged him closer. Ever closer. Which only made his head spin because he hadn't even realized she'd clutched him there. But Zeus was happy to comply, lurching forward to join the tip of his cock with her waiting mouth.

As long as he lived, he would never forget the precious moments of agonized anticipation. The sight of her tongue-slicked lips opening wide to encase part of his body...

The sublime ecstasy once the moment was realized.

The experience of watching his dagger, his bodkin, his penis, phallus, pr-prick—to use her terms—disappear past her lips...

The feel of the tongue he'd only barely begun to taste now tasting him. Licking, if not with skill, then with artless abandon.

Her touch bathed away every lingering hurt, physical and emotional. She made him a new man.

When her motions altered from licking and exploring to sucking, to drawing him so deeply, so fiercely, inside Zeus felt the wash of acceptance in every particle of his being, he worried he was about to embarrass himself —again.

And that would never do.

He slipped his hand from beneath hers and brought both to her temples. Tunneling his fingers through her hair, he took hold of her scalp and gently pulled her head back.

Open-mouthed, she released him and his nearly sucked-dry staff emerged, red and thick and shining from her depths.

Blazes! He wanted to thrust back inside and come for a sennight.

Had to do something quick before the stirring in his ballocks came spewing out on another unplanned, ungallant display.

She gazed up at him in the darkening room, face flushed, hair in a tangle over the arm of the settee. "Why?" It was a whisper. "Why did you stop me? I believe I found it rather enjoyable." And sounded totally surprised by that admission.

"Because, my sweet, 'tis your turn now."

"My turn?"

While she was all soft and subdued and submissive, he took up her hand and scooted backward, trailing their intertwined fingers over one beaded breast, past the thin muslin gathered at her waist, and to her naked abdomen. Where he paused. Waited. Then said huskily, "It's your turn to touch yourself."

"Zeus. I don't..." She protested halfheartedly, but she didn't fight him when he guided her hand the rest of the way to the juncture of her legs.

Didn't do anything more than give a slight wiggle to her hips, a little sigh of surrender.

"Here now, we'll do it together." Zeus allowed her a moment. When she slowly nodded, he worked her fingertips just inside the swollen folds. Then, with his fingers still directing hers, he fluttered them up and down.

Though the nails that had seized his arse earlier now clutched at his shoulder, she didn't shy away. Not from him nor the sensations he wrought forth, the hitch to her breath, the flinching of her pelvis, both indicating how receptive, how responsive she was.

"I— Oh!"

At the awkwardness that threatened when she touched a part of her body she'd only before ever grazed through a washing cloth, Juliet admonished herself. There was no need to freeze, to fear the unknown. Not anymore. Because it was Zeus taking her there. Showing her something new.

Showing her...

As the fury outside waned, stormy day turning to peaceful night, the tempest inside wept harder and understanding dawned. "I'm wet! Slick..." *Sticky and wanton and yearning for your possession.*

“You are indeed.” He released her hand but kept up the sensuous torture with his own. “Dampened.”

“Your...dampening ‘praiseworthy actions’.”

“Exactly. Your body preparing the way for mine.”

And with that he leaned in between her thighs for the most intimate of kisses. After plying her with several, Juliet comprehended. “Your delightful tongue!”

“Mmmm.”

Her hips bucked against his mouth and she embraced the rolling waves that grew with each languid lick and furious flick. She craved that other part of him though. The one she’d just touched and tasted. And was now ready to claim for her own. “Zeus?”

“Hmm?”

“Would you bring your conversational skills to my mouth?”

He raised his head to murmur, “Aye, my lady.”

With one last lingering kiss to her core, he drifted up her body and nudged her lips open. Acquainting her with her own flavor, he seduced her all over again.

As HER TONGUE CHASED HIS, Zeus stroked his hand down her cleft and smeared her essence over his shaft. Fisting the thick column, he placed his crown to her curls and glided along her swollen folds, skimming over the entrance and the tiny nub he'd coaxed earlier, until he heard her breath catch, felt her teeth sink into his tongue.

Knowing he'd found the place and pressure, the exact nuance between tantalize and tease she needed to gain release, he continued caressing her with his cock and (once he'd retracted his tongue) charming her with words and whispers. She writhed beneath him, and just when concern over her injured leg prodded him, she whimpered once and melted into the settee. Her moan of sublime satisfaction breezing past his ears.

Recognizing how being with this woman made him richer than possessing any amount of money or property, Zeus inched his fingers from his excessively patient erection and spread her open. He eased inside the snug, welcoming passage that rippled around him, pausing once in place to bring his face to hers.

Resting on his elbows above her, his body shaking with the continued effort of restraint, Zeus stared into her eyes. "My lady, my *wife*."

At her nod, he thrust home, past the final resistance and into her heart.

"JULIET?" Wivy's voice intruded some time later, reluctantly it sounded to Juliet, through the locked door. A trio of sharp raps followed. "Juliet! I so regret disturbing you, but we have visitors. More precisely, *you* have visitors."

"Visitors?" The man beside her roused himself to murmur. She saw his eyes blink open to startlingly swift realization of their surroundings.

Ensconced snugly in his arms, Juliet had been watching Zeus sleep. Awash in the aftermath of his physical loving, in the surety of their emotional bond, she'd been unwilling to succumb to the lure of slumber.

Moonlight angled in from the open windows. The storm's fury totally spent, the ground sated—as was her curiosity about the male form, for the moment—crickets echoed her contented feelings, merrily chirping their welcome to another night. Another night which heralded another day, neither of which she need fear any longer. Not now that her Marriage Scheme had come to a splendid conclusion.

But would Zeus share in her certainty? Or would he have regrets? Would he decry what they'd just done? Now that he'd "slept" on things, would doubts creep forth, stealing into the mind of this proud warrior she hoped to claim as her own kingly knight forevermore?

Nay, for he smiled and pressed a tender kiss to her cheek. "My lady? It appears as though we have our first guests to welcome."

It did indeed.

His actions and words easily banishing any speck of pitch-kettledness, Juliet slowly eased herself upright. Toward Wivy, she called, "Guests? At this hour?"

Turning to Zeus, who hadn't budged from his sprawled position behind her, Juliet felt her dratted cheeks heat. "We certainly aren't dressed to receive callers, now are we?"

Giving her nude form an exaggerated leer, Zeus quipped, "We certainly aren't dressed at all."

"Aye!" Wivy responded in the midst of their mirth. "The vicar. I wasn't going to disturb you, but he insists he must be on his way soon and he refuses to leave without seeing you."

"The vicar?" That was unpredicted.

"Arranged by Mr. Hastings. Come to perform a wedding, dare I hope?"

A wedding?

"Tell him we'll be down directly," Zeus answered loudly before she had a chance to.

His countenance completely solemn, only the glint in his eyes betraying the laughter they'd just shared, Zeus stood and bowed before her, in all his naked majesty. "My lady?" He rose and held his arm toward her, palm up. "If you'll have me?"

Forever. Heart pounding ferociously at the commitment she was about to make, confident in her decision as she'd never thought to be, Juliet placed her hand in his. "I'll have you forever, Zeus Jupiter."

"Minx. That stays between us." After giving her hand a squeeze, Zeus released her to snatch his buckskins from the floor.

"Ah..." His head whipped to and fro. "My shirt? I seem to recall displacing it earlier. Have you any idea where it got off to?"

Remembering exactly where he'd left it, where she'd first inhaled his strong scent, Juliet pointed toward the screen. "I do indeed."

Zeus quickly retreated that direction. But, lovely man, he took the time to retrieve her dress as well and toss it to her before donning his own attire.

"Perhaps..." she said archly, tugging her dress overhead and immediately proposing once she emerged, "I could interest you in another exchange?"

His face turned speculative and he paused in his efforts to stuff in his shirt. "What would you have of me? You've already stript me raw." Though he didn't seem to mind overly much, given how one side of his mouth quirked upward. "Turned my expectations and my life on their ear since I stepped foot into your shaky, sodden abode."

"Oh how you go on," she teased, unable to subdue the spark of pure joy that flashed through her knowing she could. Tease him, that was. "I'll grant you blind obedience in public..." Juliet let that dangle temptingly between them, "*if* I can call you Zeus Jupiter in private."

He growled. He groaned. He grinned full-out. "For blind obedience, I'll suffer through it."

"You're such a dear!" She watched him tug on his Hessians, forgoing his woolen stockings in his haste. A glance toward her discarded pale pink one had her cheeks heating all over again. "Now where did my slipper get off to?"

She required that and her crutch in order to retrieve her undergarments strewn between here and yonder and the corner where she'd hid—and first glimpsed heaven: Zeus' chest. Pity he'd had to cover it up. But the tingly, tender sensations between her nude thighs reminded her *she* still had much to cover up as well.

"You won't need your slipper," he informed her, and proceeded to gather her in his arms, ignoring her shriek as he advanced straight toward the door.

"Zeus! We can't go down like this!"

"Why ever not?"

"You skipped your waistcoat and tailcoat and I'm still…still *in my altogether* under my dres*mpfth*!"

His kiss muffled the protest and made away with her breath. "It matters not," he said when he raised his head. "Because directly upon completion of our abbreviated nuptials, you'll be acquainting me with your bedchamber—and before you remind me, I know it leaks. I'll shove the bed into a dry patch tonight and climb on the roof tomorrow for an inspection, after I dispatch someone to the village with a handful of coins to procure us some real and hearty food."

Gracious, he was already taking charge. How wondrous!

Balancing her against his chest, he unlocked the door and opened it a few inches for Henry who *mewed* a quick thanks and flew through the crack, fluffy tail held high. "Now *you*"—Zeus hefted her in his arms, such a delightful, protected feeling—"you behave. Or else."

Kicking her bare feet in a show of pure unconcern, Juliet wrapped one arm behind his neck and placed her lips to his ear. "Or else what?"

Zeus eased the door completely open with one elbow, sliding her carefully through before imparting, "Or else I'll tell the vicar exactly what you *aren't* wearing under that pretty dress."

"Zeus!"

EPILOGUE ~ JULIET. MEMORIES. HOME.

"WHAT'S that you're concentrating on? More modifications to the building plans?"

Zeus had wondered how long it would take his bride of two months to ask. He'd made a great show of preparing the nib, uncapping the ink and sighing in audible satisfaction upon the completion of each word.

He tugged her onto one leg and leaned back. "Your first official reading lesson, which just happens to coincide with my lesson in Revised Values." Though they'd covered individual letters, life had intervened since he'd made his promise, kept him from honoring it as soon as he'd wished.

Between spending nearly every waking moment together, and waking her in the middle of the night to create more of them, plus paying off creditors, visiting tenants and working with Olivia and her man to secure the necessary workforce to adequately improve the ramshackle estates, "hectic" hardly described the past few weeks.

Glorious weeks.

Inhaling the delicate scent of the bounty in his arms, Zeus extended one hand to slide the foolscap toward them. He put his finger beneath the first word. "This one, I believe you know?"

After studying it a moment, she looked at him in surprise. "That's me. Juliet."

A broad grin widened his cheeks. "So it is." Allowing his finger to track each word, he read, "*Things I Value—Juliet. Memories. Home.* It's a far cry different from my previous list."

"I approve!" She slung her arms around his neck. "Care to share the former?"

"Mum was on it, of course. So was Amherst, as were time and money." But time with his bride, jointly discussing how best to spend his money, had swiftly led to a revelation: Neither of those was worth spit unless he splurged them on things that mattered.

"Want to hear my list? Then you can show me how to write it."

She scooted off and stood over his shoulder while he dipped the pen and prepared to inscribe her words. "I await your pleasure, my dear," he prompted when she remained silent.

"My husband." He wrote, adding *Zeus* in parentheses when she requested it, saying that was definitely one she wanted to learn.

"Henry." He penned with a smile, glancing over at the ball of fluff sleeping (and shedding) atop yesterday's waistcoat.

"Wivy, Jacks and our other new friends and servants." His pen flowed as she dictated. He knew how she missed those companions who'd remained near Duffield while they'd traveled to London to meet with the architect who would oversee the construction of their new home at Amherst.

"Our...little...Jupiter."

The second her words registered, the ink smeared. The J lurched off the page. Zeus dropped the pen and snared his wife. "You're with child?"

Roses bloomed on her cheeks. "I believe so."

He stood and whirled her around in a circle that encompassed the entirety of their rented rooms. "You've made me the happiest of men, my lady. But if you think any son of mine is going to carry a blighted name such as—"

Her lips at his ear stopped the tirade. "Would you agree to James? Or Jane?"

"Aye, I would."

"Then put me down, Mr. Tanner, and I'll trade you my two stockings for your shirt and buckskins."

Author's Note

I really hope you enjoyed *Lady Scandal*. This book, more than anything else I've written, tends to polarize readers – they either adore it or think it's wretched. Filthy. (Yeah, I've had more than a couple scathing reviews deriding this little story.) The humor has *not* appealed to everyone.

I think it's downright funny, but then I remember watching and cracking up over *Benny Hill* by myself when I was a kid and, for some reason, I kind of doubt that the adult-oriented British sitcom may have been common viewing for many other Texas youngsters. :-)

My dad says I get my sense of humor from my grandmother. Which is funny by itself because I remember her holding a Bible in her hand more often than not, so some of the salty stories and tales I've heard about—or from—her take a bit of imagination. Fortunately, I've got that in spades, and my wonderful grandmother is who first introduced me to romance books. Even when my mother said I was too young to read them, Grandma would "pre-approve" the early Harlequin romances she had stashed under her bed and let me read the ones that didn't have too much physical interaction.

Obviously, I've gone way beyond that restriction now, and I love writing sexy stories that hopefully make people smile.

Later this year, my *Roaring Rogues Regency Shapeshifters* are coming back! I'm super excited about that.

Meanwhile, if you're ready to read more, swipe on for an introduction to another fun and steamy Regency love story…one with a very special place in my heart.

SEDUCTIVE SILENCE
INTRODUCTION

While *Lady Scandal* was always intended to be a flirty, borderline-erotic Regency novella, things took a different turn on my next story.

Though my *Mistress in the Making* series started out the same way, it soon blossomed into an extended-length, more emotional story of true hardship and ultimately finding that special person who makes you a better version of yourself. Of course, it's also brimming with steamy scenes and my trademark humor too (but no salty scones—I promise!).

Thea, raised on the fringes of London society, is left destitute when her unromantic husband dies, and soon it's a nightly battle to fill her belly–one she often loses to the two mice, George and Charlotte, she shares her hovel of a rented room with. In such a dire situation, who among us wouldn't at least *consider* becoming a kept convenient? Especially when Thea's friend, a long-time courtesan, makes it sound so much better than starving? *And* has a particular gentleman in mind…

For Daniel–a marquis who struggles to hide his stammering difficulty (taught by his ruthless father he was less of a man, of a *person*, because of it), the thought of seeking out a new mistress would leave his tongue tied in knots–if it wasn't already.

After their first (not-quite) intimate night together, Daniel tries his hand at penning a letter to the lovely Thea, and soon the two embark on a fun, flirty exchange that was a sheer joy to write. Thea, especially, surprising me with a racy sense of humor she'd kept hidden till then.

The story also incorporates Daniel's fascination with orreries—something I learned of quite by accident, and only recently. Solar system miniatures...how wonderful to be surprised by learning of something that's been around for centuries that was completely brand new to my awareness!

And while completing their impassioned journey took far longer than I wished, these two have lived on in my heart more than other characters who have found their happily ever after. Like Daniel, I sometimes have trouble speaking, only from a musculature standpoint not because of severe stuttering, and for an author who uses dictation software to write, that's frustrating on so many levels. I think I may relate to him more than other characters (so much more, that I think I've developed a crush—shhh! We'll not tell Thea or Mr. Lyons about that, all right?).

The first part of Daniel and Thea's journey, ***Seductive Silence,*** is available as a FREE ebook from most vendors. Turn the page for the blurb and an excerpt of their first meeting...

SEDUCTIVE SILENCE BLURB AND EXCERPT

Seductive Silence
Mistress in the Making, Book 1

Pestered by a persistent stammer, a Regency lord must find a way to woo his new mistress without words. He just hopes she can hear what's in his heart.

Lord Tremayne has a problem. He stammers like a fool—at least that's what he learned from his father's constant criticism and punishing hand. Daniel now hides his troubles, limiting his speech and getting by with a few close friends. His well-fought privacy is all for naught when he goes looking for a new mistress and finds a delightful young woman who makes him, of all people, want to spout poetry. He thought he had a problem before? Avoiding meaningless dinner prattle is nothing compared to the challenge of winning the heart of his new lady lust.

Recently widowed and increasingly poor, Thea's been reduced to sharing her rented room with rodents and arguing over every morsel (the mice usually win). When a friend suggests an alliance of the most intimate sort, Thea's reluctantly intrigued. But given her lackluster marriage, she doubts her ability to entice an experienced man. The considerate, if quiet, Lord Tremayne attracts her mightily, so she sets aside her misgivings. That is, until Thea realizes she's about to break the cardinal rule of mistressing—that of falling for her new protector.

Seductive Silence Excerpt

At a party of the demimonde, where the two are meeting for the first time...

"And Lord Tremayne?" Dorothea squeaked out hurriedly. "Which one is he?"

Sarah acknowledged her cook, indicated she'd be over in a moment, then scanned the crowd.

Dorothea prayed Sarah would point out someone other than the men she'd particularly noticed. There were others, a small, boisterous group of males lingering across the hall in another room, tumblers in hand, but there were as many or more "ladies" in their midst and not a one of the men had cast so much as an inquiring glance her direction. "I thought you said there were only going to be a dozen men here tonight."

Dorothea's count was up to fifteen at least.

"That's what I thought until receiving Penry's note this afternoon. A few others got wind of our gathering and begged invitations." Sarah took Dorothea's arm and casually strolled until she could see into the next room.

Dorothea tried not to be overly critical, tried to remember what awaited her at home: a moldy potato, mice groats—would that her options proliferated as fast as George and Charlotte's "leavings"—and grabby Grimmett. She tried to be grateful, thankful for the opportunity of tonight. But as she evaluated the men present, the ones not melded at the hips to their mistresses already, she had to admit not a one of them appealed to her on the physical level she'd secretly yearned for.

"La, that man," Sarah said finally. "I told Tremayne supper was served at nine and not a moment later. And still he runs late."

Upon realizing none of the unpalatable choices before her were the man in question, a surge of relief swept through Dorothea. Mayhap the tardy Lord Tremayne would appeal after all.

Do you recognize the significance of that? a part of her brain seemed to ask.

He's *late*, some imp emphasized.

Late, something her "late" spouse would never, ever have tolerated. Too easily she could recall the disapproving glares should his breakfast, luncheon, dinner—or heaven forfend, afternoon tea—be placed before him even one second beyond the strike of the hour.

My, oh my, Lord Tremayne was tardy. Dorothea smiled, predisposed to like him already.

At twelve minutes past nine, Daniel presented his tardy carcass at the home he'd been invited to, doffed his hat, coat, cane and gloves, relinquishing them to the overly officious butler, and prayed he hadn't made a mistake in coming tonight.

At the pointedly assessing look the man gave his jaw—insolent fellow!—Daniel's fingers automatically followed. So he encountered scruff instead of skin. What of it? He'd ordered Crowley, his valet, to trim and refine his whiskers in lieu of shaving them off.

Better to disguise the bruise and scars than to scare her away before ever opening his mouth. *Her* being the woman he suffered through this ordeal to meet.

"My lord, delighted you deigned to join us," the butler said with a haughty air that indicated he took his position very seriously. "Dinner is being held on your account, so if you would…"

The man set off at a marching pace before the first syllable of Daniel's "Lead on," made it past his lips.

No out-of-the-way narrow nook for Penry's lovely light-skirt, Daniel saw, the home he was escorted through being as genteel and grand as anything one would expect to find in Mayfair. Only they weren't in Mayfair, the upper echelon of abodes, but a neighborhood or three away.

"Here we are, my lord."

Nodding his thanks to the impertinent fellow, Daniel paused before entering the formal dining room, keeping out of sight of most its occupants. Though the space was absurdly large, a slightly low ceiling coupled with the crowd inhabiting it gave the room an intimate, almost cozy air. Elaborate candelabra spaced evenly over the table's surface ensured adequate light—a sort of subdued, shadowed light that invited one to lean their head toward their closest companion for a romantic *tête-à-tête*.

He cast his gaze back the way they'd just come and unease threatened to crawl through him.

Penry certainly hadn't spared any expense outfitting his mistress, had he?

Daniel hadn't yet seen the lodgings he'd secured for his potential paramour, wanting a fresh start in fresh surroundings with a—hopefully—fresh woman. He'd had his man of affairs take care of it and hadn't bothered to inspect the townhouse himself. Hadn't his man assured him it was just the thing?

The nip of unease promised to metamorphize into an onslaught, fixing him—and his neck muscles in place.

'Tis nothing, he assured himself. Only a willing wren of a widow in need of protection and your pipe in need of her attention. Three fortifying breaths later, he braved crossing the threshold.

Excellent.

Everyone was seated. Just as he'd hoped. Less chance of getting tangled in the trap of idle chatter before supper if people were hungrily anticipating it.

Silently acknowledging the greetings he received from the group at large, Daniel smiled and nodded at several acquaintances as he made his way around the giant oval table to this evening's hostess to make his apologies. He wouldn't put it past Penry to have purchased the huge slab for the occasion—and for the occasion of plowing into his mistress on top of it after everyone went home.

Penry sometimes talked a little too freely about his lusty interludes with the serene brunette. Ready for his own lusty interlude, Daniel scanned the women present, more than a little curious as to the identity of the well-hyped Widow Hurwell.

Penry had teased him with enough hints of subtle beauty and true refinement to pique his interest. But it was hearing of her strained circumstances that had ultimately tipped the scales and caused his carriage wheels to roll this way tonight. No money meant no options, and Daniel was desperate enough in his own right to take advantage of her situation, desperate enough to at least put himself forward. If she was truly as cultured and untarnished as he'd been led to believe, some lucky man would snatch her up and it might as well be him.

"Forgive me," he said to Penry's Sarah, coming up to her and proffering a slight bow, knowing he owed her his sincere apologies for his tardiness but unable to stop himself from avidly inspecting the woman by her side. She was the only female he didn't recognize and the only person who looked more than a little out of place, discounting the pup at the far end who gazed with his mouth agape toward the arched doorway Daniel had just entered through.

In the muted candlelight, she shone like an undiscovered jewel, her wealth of dark hair piled and looped on the back of her head in a manner quite at odds with the simplicity of her dress. But he cared not to analyze her attire for the faint stirring in his loins boded well indeed.

Faint? Putting to rest any concerns he had about not being attracted to her, at the thought of bedding the lovely widow, his body stirred more than a dead man's falling down a ravine—which is what Daniel started to think he'd been for staying with Louise for so long. Dead to any finer sense.

Determinedly, he fixed his gaze on the frowning Sarah. He started to carefully explain his fabricated, rehearsed excuse for being late. His mouth not yet open, already the tension climbed up his neck and squeezed inward—

Not now! he wanted to rail.

But Penry's woman unknowingly saved him.

"Do sit down, Lord Tremayne. I'm grateful you decided to finally grace us with your presence," she told him archly, gesturing to the lone empty seat at the table which, not coincidentally, was next to the woman he had hopes of claiming. "But I've held back supper long enough. Hopkins," she called out to a servant hovering at the ready, "tell Cook the first course may be brought in. *Finally*."

"Yes, madam."

A frisson of awareness swelled through Dorothea the moment the latecomer came into view. When Sarah called him Tremayne, the subtle tingling became more of a lightning spike.

Of what, Dorothea couldn't say. The gruff-looking man didn't appeal exactly, but he most definitely *attracted*—both her attention and greetings from many of the men present.

"Glad to see that munsons muffler didn't lay you out for long."

Munsons muffler?

"Nay. Not our man—way to work it till the ringer!"

"Jolly good show, Tremayne."

What? Did he perform in some venue? What an odd occupation for a peer. But apparently, instead of diminishing his standing, it only served to enhance it.

Yet...as he surveyed the room and his gaze alit upon her, she didn't think Lord Tremayne needed any more enhancement when a surge of—

What exactly? Interest? Appreciation? Speculation? A surge of *something* foreign to her experience came into his eyes, something hot and banked glittering from the depths of deep amber. Being the recipient of such focused potency drove some part of her to contemplate jumping from her seat to proclaim she was ready to retire with him straightaway.

The other part of her, the heretofore sensible part that seemed to be undergoing a most peculiar change—into sultry?—commanded her lips to curve into a welcoming smile, her melting body to stay put and her eyes to narrow (she feared losing them if they opened any wider) as he made his way to the available chair next to hers and she undeniably drank him in.

He was a big man, powerfully built yet somehow tamed by the trappings he wore—a rich brown tailcoat over a waistcoat in a muted burgundy stripe, with tan buckskins below. A cream-colored cravat, meticulously tied, and rebelliously straight hair. Rebellious, because all the rage was tousled curls for men and sausage ringlets for the ladies, as she'd been informed when Sarah's abigail had tended to hers.

She liked the silky-looking, thick strands adorning Lord Tremayne's well-shaped head (Mr. Hurwell's had been rather narrow; his head, that was. His hair, somewhat lank.). She liked Lord Tremayne's confident air and strong-looking body too.

She especially liked the way he smelled, now that he was close enough to inhale, clean and spicy, with just a hint of the outdoors.

What she couldn't yet claim to like was his beard. And how he appeared intimidating beneath the bristle, all hard, flexing jaw and tendon-filled neck—she'd glimpsed a couple inches below his chin and above the cravat when he cocked his head in a peculiar stretch just before taking possession of his chair.

And until she had reason to like *him*, rather than land herself further into the suds, Dorothea knew she'd bide her time. Wait and discern what manner of man he truly was before agreeing to proceed with a liaison between them.

But oh, how she liked the flood of warmth that beset her every limb when he joined her beneath the table, his long, powerful body coming within inches of hers as he brought his chair forward...how she admired his forearm encased in expensive superfine she'd never thought to view up close—much less consider touching, as he reached for his wine...

Taking advantage of the slight commotion when several servants began tromping in carrying silver-domed trays, Daniel dodged further introductions by settling himself next to the woman he suspected he was here to meet.

And to bed.

Briefly her eyes flicked to his and a ghost of a smile touched her lips before it faded like a breeze. But the damage was done—one covert, up-close, lash-shrouded glance and all he could do was gape and goggle.

Soft tendrils of her luxuriant midnight hair framed a heart-shaped face. The flickering candlelight caused shadows to dance over her slightly angular nose and jaw. She was a mite thin for his tastes, but any hint of hardness in her features was belied by the bow-shaped mouth that commanded his attention.

So easily he imagined those plump lips against his, parted and welcoming, where he would sample the passion he hoped was packaged inside this delightful exterior. He'd like to see her dark hair rid of its pins, his fingers tangled against her scalp as he guided her lips lower...

A hot spike of lust wound through him and Daniel smiled.

Rescuing Sarah's little widow would prove no hardship. Indeed, could the timing have been any more fortuitous? At long last, his long lance would undoubtedly sleep snug and satisfied, and, finally, he'd *sleep*. Snugged against the lithe body he suspected resided beneath the atrocious dress.

Closer now, he couldn't help but notice its shortcomings. Her olive gown had obviously seen better days. A thin fichu was tucked into the low, squared-off bosom, concealing her attributes completely. After the overtly stimulating attire Louise typically wore, the widow's outfit was almost puritan in its severity. Puritan yet provocative...encouraging visions of divesting her of the drab layers and uncovering what lay beneath.

Giving his body a moment to relax, he turned to his meal. A task which proved surprisingly difficult when, moments later, he was fully aware of her slight wrist grappling with the overdone mutton on her plate. His was already neatly severed. So with nothing more than a lift of one brow and an inquiring *Hmmm?* that had her pausing in her efforts, he deftly switched their plates, quickly sliced her serving and had them swapped back before anyone took notice.

A well-timed bite between his choppers ensured all he had to do was nod after her quiet but appreciative thanks and he was off—inspecting her again (for it was a significantly more enjoyable endeavor than chewing overcooked mutton).

And so it went. Most of the table's occupants engaging in light, meaningless banter with the lovely Mrs. Hurwell chiming in as appropriate.

Daniel found himself more than pleased.

She answered promptly and with an undercurrent of wit not everyone circling the table seemed privy to. Her responses, while intelligent and entertaining—to him at least—were concise, he noted with no little degree of appreciation. Neither did she instigate conversation but only responded when posed a direct query.

Exquisite. Could he have asked for better?

Lord Tremayne's admiring analysis and pleasure over Dorothea's lack of verbosity would have most certainly been mitigated had he but known how she battled the inner longing to turn to him and inquire fifty and one assorted things: Was he always this quiet? Did he truly like the glazed shoe leather on his plate? (He must, he'd downed it with nary a blink.) Which poets did he find particularly fascinating? And what in heaven's name was a munsons muffler?

The servants brought out another course, this one glazed duck—she thought. It was a bit difficult to tell as the poor bird was so raw it was practically still swimming. Foregoing the foul fowl altogether, Dorothea picked nimbly through the macaroni noodles—they seemed safe enough, if a trifle undercooked—and allowed herself to admit what she *really* wanted to ask: Why had Lord Tremayne neglected to shave his chin whiskers?

Was he growing out his beard or did he not care enough about meeting her to bother? And did he always smell so nice? (A curious combination of cloves and honeysuckle that made her want to forego the filling noodles and lick him instead. Shameful, she knew, but the urge was undeniable.) What did he do with his days? Did he want *her* for his mistress? Had he any inkling yet, one way or the other? How often might he visit? *Was he married?*

Heavens to Hertfordshire, but just thinking of everything she wanted to ask him was enough to keep her mute. Well, her chaotic thoughts *and* Sarah's counsel: *Take your cue from him.*

So this was a man who wanted quiet? She shoved aside the pang of disappointment at not finding a boon companion in her first foray into the demimonde.

Then she fortified her resolve because *quiet* she could do; wedded to Mr. Hurwell, she'd lived in it long enough.

How soon could they leave? Blazing ballocks, but he'd guillotine Penry if he'd arranged some drawn-out shadow play as he'd done the last time Daniel consented to attend one of these asinine public affairs. That one had been years ago at Sarah's standard-strumpet townhouse, before his friend had invested more than common sense recommended in his high flyer's accommodations and purchased her this near mansion. Louise had been enamored with the salacious shadow play and once they'd returned to her lodgings, had wanted him to perform a strip behind a sheet, backlit by the fire, for her amusement (he'd sooner swim the Thames—*bound* in a sheet).

He cringed at the memory. Thank God she'd found another protector, some American captain more flush in his pockets than his crown office had swept her off to his ship. She'd sent round a perfumed note before they'd sailed to make sure Daniel knew she wasn't pining for him. He grunted. Not hardly. Who would pine for that bird-witted bird of paradise —when Paradise of another kind waited in the chair beside him?

A good night's sleep after a good round of frisking! He'd sing if he could, bellow out his delight—

What? Yammer out the tune of your faults?

By damn, he'd nearly forgotten.

A stunned, strangled groan worked its way free of his throat.

When she looked at him directly, the very source of his amazed consternation, a puzzled expression on her face, Daniel realized he'd gone practically the entire meal without uttering a word.

Gad, he was an arse.

The first part of Daniel and Thea's journey, ***Seductive Silence,*** is available as a FREE ebook from most vendors. What are you waiting for? Grab it!

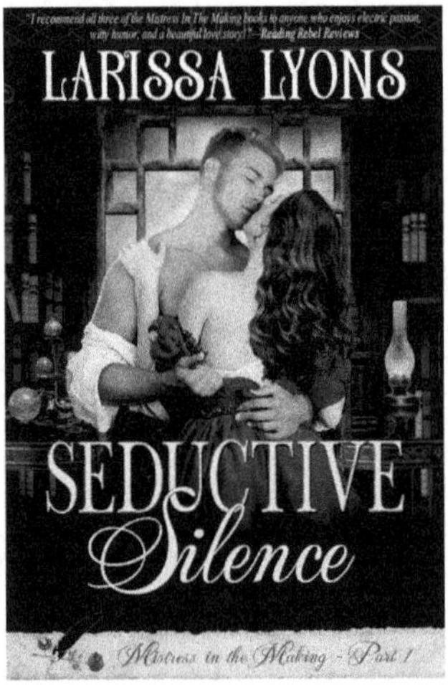

ABOUT LARISSA

HUMOR. HEARTFELT EMOTION. & HUNKS.

Larissa writes steamy regencies and sexy contemporaries, blending heartfelt emotion with doses of laugh-out-loud humor. Her heroes are strong men with a weakness for the right woman.

Avoiding housework one word at a time (thanks in part to her super-helpful herd of cats >^..^<), Larissa adores brownies, James Bond, and her husband. She's been a clown, a tax analyst, and a pig castrator (!) but nothing satisfies quite like seeing the entertaining voices in her head come to life on the page.

Writing around some health challenges and computer limitations, it's a while between releases, but stick with her...she's working on the next one.

Learn more at LarissaLyons.com.

facebook.com/AuthorLarissaLyons
instagram.com/larissa_lyons_author
amazon.com/author/larissalyons
bookbub.com/authors/larissa-lyons
goodreads.com/larissalyons

MORE BANG-UP REGENCIES BY LARISSA

Coming Soon

Ensnared by Innocence (Summer 2021)

Oh, the angst! Changing into a lion isn't all fur and games.

Lord Blakely doesn't have time for innocents. His carnal appetites lean toward experienced women, ones who accommodate his need for frequent—and frequently wild—sex. Especially as The Change draws near.

The uniquely captivating female...

Lady Francine Montfort may have led a sheltered life till her parents' untimely demise but that doesn't mean she's ignorant. Neither is she blind to the conniving ways of her persistent aunt, who's determined to marry Francine off for her own selfish gain. Forced to drastic measures to avoid the wretched woman's scheming, Francine concocts her own masterful plan.

But she'll need to enlist the assistance of a powerful man of the ton to help her enact it. Dare she approach the Marquis of Blakely—the sinfully alluring lord who inspires all manner of illicit thoughts and fantasies? Though she doubts he realizes it, he's already rescued her once. Might he do so again?

...who just might entice him to risk everything.

When Lady Francine, the epitome of innocence, requests he pose as her betrothed, Blakely knows he should handily refuse. He's baffled when unfamiliar, protective urges make themselves known, tempting him to agree.

Alas, it's fast approaching the season when Blakely loses all control. Either Francine satisfies his sexual appetites or he'll be forced to reveal his beastly side. And that will never do. Not now that he's come to care for the intrepid chit.

Note to Readers: This love story between two people contains a lot of sizzle, including one ménage scene that gets rather...growly.

Standalone ~HEA ~ Book 1 - Roaring Rogues Regency Shifters

AVAILABLE NOW

Mistress in the Making Trilogy

A fun, emotionally satisfying, steamy tale told in three parts: Seductive Silence, Lusty Letters, and Daring Declarations.

Seductive Silence , Part 1

Lord Tremayne has a problem. He stammers like a fool—at least that's what he learned from his father's constant criticism and punishing hand. Daniel now hides his troubles by barley saying anything. But then he goes looking for a new mistress and finds a delightful young woman who makes him, of all people, want to spout poetry. He thought he had a problem before? Avoiding meaningless dinner prattle is nothing compared to the challenge of winning the heart of his new lady lust.

Lusty Letters, Part 2

Thea's fascinating new protector has secrets—several. Hesitant to destroy her newfound circumstances, she stifles her longing to know everything about the powerfully built—and frustratingly quiet—Marquis. But then his naughty notes start to appear, full of humor and wit, and Thea realizes she's about to break the cardinal rule of mistressing—that of falling for her new protector. *Egad.*

Daring Declarations, Part 3

An evening at the opera could prove Lord Tremayne's undoing when he and his lovely new paramour cross paths with his sister and brother-in-law. Introducing one's socially unacceptable strumpet to his stunned family is *never* done. But Daniel does it anyway. And it might just be the best decision he's ever made, for Thea's quickly become much more than a mistress—and it's time he told her so.

Miss Isabella Thaws a Frosty Lord

Blind from a young age, a Regency heroine risks her overbearing father's displeasure by attending a house party, never dreaming she'll meet a formidable lord who will discover all her secrets and still want her for his own.

Top Pick! "This entertaining read conjured up the atmosphere and exquisitely formal dance of manners so beloved in Jane Austen's books... I am enchanted by the grace and artful wordplay that accompanies this tale."
ELF, Night Owl Reviews

"I love the way that the book reads as if it were written in Regency times. I'm a fan of Carla Kelly Regency romances and I was in the mood for another story of that caliber. I definitely got that with *Miss Isabella Thaws a Frosty Lord.*" *EKDuncan*

LARISSA'S BOOKLIST

Historicals by Larissa Lyons

ROARING ROGUES REGENCY SHIFTERS

Ensnared by Innocence (Summer 2021)

Deceived by Desire (Fall 2021)

Tamed by Temptation (2022)

MISTRESS IN THE MAKING series (Complete)

Seductive Silence

Lusty Letters

Daring Declarations

FUN & SEXY REGENCY ROMANCE

Lady Scandal

A SWEETLY SPICY REGENCY

Miss Isabella Thaws a Frosty Lord

Contemporaries by Larissa Lynx

SEXY CONTEMPORARY ROMANCE

Renegade Kisses

Starlight Seduction

POWER PLAYERS HOCKEY series

*My Two-Stud Stand**

*Her Three Studs**

The Stud Takes a Stand (2022)

**Her Hockey Studs - print version*

SHORT STORY STEAMY INSTALOVE

A Heart for Adam...& Rick!

Braving Donovan's

No Guts, No 'Gasms

Literary Madness!

CPSIA information can be obtained
at www.ICGtesting.com
Printed in the USA
BVHW041541150721
611947BV00028B/802

9 781949 426250